MASTERFUL

AC/E
ACCIÓN CULTURAL
ESPAÑOLA

MASTERFUL
Rubén Martín Giráldez

~

Translated by Peter Kahn

QUANTUM PROSE

So, in whose head could it possibly have entered to think that your Master would fantasize about no longer using the Spanish language when he owns both you and the language in which you grieve? You grieve. Isn't it an open secret that Spanish –peninsular variety at least– has finally begun to be used unabashedly as an emetic in certain European countries? It's true that only I am to blame for that, and I shouldn't go around wasting time on couplets seasoned with the salt and poison of my youth, but does what I do now really concern you considering the short amount of time my post has left to devote to my vocation? If it were up to you, you'd put a cage on my mouth and that would be the end of that. Isn't it time to speak fluently again? Do I have to keep using this languagio? Will I always be a listener and nothing more? This is a regency, an office, the greatest position of responsibility your subjects have ever invented for you, and not a pastime, you tell me. What has brought me to this, chatterer and arrogant, and yet completely paralyzed from the waist down? Go on: give the orator something to drink, seeing as how you're incapable of conversation or responding to a single one of the questions that more out of courtesy than curiosity I've asked you; because while you're talking, while I'm talking, I'm constantly aware of my weight, my physical defects and ordinary corporeal miseries (nothing serious: an electrical reflex in my right lung—so it's not my heart, but rather its escort—perforations in the globus pallidus, dry eyes, the tongue burned by acids: the usual for a person, to be expected for a relic or for a king), which can only be replenished by liquids. Do you hear me, or are you too distracted playing with the folds of my tunic? I'd forgotten what it's like to limit myself to idle villanelles without overtightening the knots on the torture rack, like it or not: it's so easy to release these words into another ether and then see who has the gumption to catch up to us. How irksome the truth is when it's not our own. If I made myself tell the truth, it would get stuck in my snout, with all the justification in the world, and I would immediately be exposed to all kinds of reproaches, or even worse, since I'm not paid for my tidiness, nor for my inclination towards a job well done or my good intentions, in the position I hold, but rather for my *savoir faire.* Do you know how much money Obedience invests to guarantee the savoir faire of thousands of people under its care? Do you know what *savoir* means and how to faire it? Look at me, you; look at me, don't let me out of your sight or, if not, how do you expect to read in my face the face you should put on? What's the point of me putting into writing this melancholic language, a tongue that has lost all its tenacity? You know full well that I no longer write; what I have here is a very good voice and no ability for singing, and that is why I'd never reduce myself to a reproducible testimony of my gaucherie. And that's not for fear of being judged, because I managed to escape that farce one lucky day. There are many differences between what I used to do and what I've decided to do today; before, I would have begun by looking for some kind of presumptuous ejaculation, like:

> Where Mozart wrote *fortissimo*, we are obliged not to recreate a *fortissimo* with the sonorous possibilities of the eighteenth century, but rather to interpret it with the means we have today for playing a *fortissimo* that rises to its full potential.
>
> *Piano Notes: The World of the Pianist*, Charles Rosen

And then I would have improvised something. But tell me, talk to me, tap into me: why does someone decide to speak, having declared they abominate the only language they actually have command over, convinced they are more or less good and content with their life, yet indifferent to yours and merciless? Convinced, did I say? A slip, but now we're not going to launch into an S/Z examination of ourselves, or are we?

It doesn't surprise me that no nation has consented to having my libelous *Masterful* translated into their language considering the state in which I've left the Spanish tongue. The impact of *Masterful* had only been having an effect for a few days when the viceprecedent informed me that Spanish had *fallen into a state of dysfunction* and that at this point it was too late to do anything else than to turn coldblooded. I asked the Viceprecedent, as nicely as I could, to kindly have the concupiscence to notify the pobulation of the badtiding. "Larvas and goebblemen: the languagio: I cerebrate that you've enjoyed it," he managed to burble before the Chamber. The sixth word he had to formulate with his hands rather than his mouth, he raspberried, the invisible tinsel remained suspended precisely where it had been emitted and the representative of the top representative of

State turned on his heels swearing on the barrel of Brent or Brand's Haide (the versions differ) and he marched off to the gulf port, leaving the stupefied Obedience stranded. This appearance officially began (that is: with a fixed and memorable image) the period of stammering in which we've been immersed for the last two years, whose fruits have rendered this servant to propose, from time to time, that he should meet with the parishioners of Mother Mimicry, for lack of a better word. Since then, we've seen some *melioration*, or that's how some of you conceive of it. I would call it *conformity*, a *plateau*. I don't feel proud. *Masterful* didn't just destroy the code that enabled us to communicate with each other: it also annihilated the history of good taste in our country. Why does it surprise you that it should be a dignitary responsible for taking the big step? After all, to resuscitate taste, it would be necessary, sometime, for this nation to take seriously the notion that our body is a temple and our mouth is its outhouse, and the most logical course to take would be to think about reconstructing the language so that we could at least lie about how clean we keep our castle, lined with skin and hair and irremediably perforated nine or ten times. We should probably be thinking of changing some things, changing what no longer works. Perhaps it's time to change languages. On the other hand, today the reader is the enemy of the poet, because the admirer (who doesn't need to read in order to admire) is the greatest obstacle and the poison-taster is the friend of both; consequently, the written word has become a kind of entertainment that satisfies other regions of the language. Whereas the prohibition against public admiration was, until a few years ago, tacit, today, thanks to new regulations and norms against bardolatry, one can't expect support from the old supporters. Furtive admiration, likewise, strikes me as being of poor quality, practiced by hearsay among afficionados and a clear signal that decorum has been repudiated. It won't be necessary for me to justify that my responsibility is as large as my salary of stadtholder, and that one or another stems from the same government, which is why it would be extremely naive to expect me to run into a bardolator without immediately notifying the proper authorities, taking into account the demonstrable importance of communication in our times. To put it another way: what is so scandalous is the inability of some people to understand my fidelity to a hand that has never bitten me. I can't say the same for the reader, my natural enemy. Happiness in the conjunction of a pair of given adjectives, for the reader, is an insult, as felicity has always been an insult to the unfortunate, so I won't beat around the bush, since my arms have already grown old. What is a reader? A reader is someone who has not written what they are reading. You might think, then, that the opposite of a reader is a writer. No. The opposite of a reader is a bardolator. Bardolator and reader, both equally despicable; ultimately, the ones and the others are minions of the ones and the others.

And then—perpetually available—there's you, the *praegustator*, our food-taster. I have nothing to be ashamed of: I delivered the last one who admired me to Ben Marcus, period. The bardolator, prince of convulsionettes, is dying to talk to the author of solar refraction but runs up against the author of his own refraction of the sun. If he had read me well, he'd know that it would behoove him more to run in the opposite direction from my mouth. The thing is, even though I can't approve of this kind of uninspired outpouring in a country so used to dodging issues by eliminating every opportunity for praise, I certainly can't pretend now that I don't understand that the laws have to be updated frequently and that the norms are only remembered when official measures are applied with appropriate pomp and circumstance. Is passing information to a lower authority considered obloquy? —It doesn't sound Spanish at all, more like Flemish jargon, obloquy, ugly patois. I can hardly be accused of *fulfilling* anything. It's not as if the bardolator, until now, were wandering loose out there without punishment or anything, as if it weren't enough to live a life of devotion to someone who disdains him. I, therefore, was fulfilling not just an obligation, but rather—and much more compellingly—a desire and even a natural inclination; what people who are even more foul-spoken than I might call a *proclivity*. Don't mind me. And that's what I came for, to say what a good person I am. I dedicate one of my last lucid nights to the proper fulfillment of the norms (does it detract in any way from a man or a king of men the fact that he wishes to dedicate his last thoughts to the laws his compatriots have created and obeyed instead of to other issues he considers inferior?); to them, I dedicate all that I have put off in my head until this day, in a serious format; in a format—thus, the delay—that is absolutely contrary to diction, or contrary to what appears to be diction, given that today I find myself stuck in a North American Mouth attempting to steal its langue and tongue. Now you laugh? Just a moment ago, abandoning our langtong didn't seem like such a bad idea to you and you added your applause to the calls for Obedience.

I would love to tell you to take it calmly: wait until the whistling subsides and swallow your last bite. But ultimately, we find ourselves, they say, in the *crépuscule* of words, and it's very hard to manage to go back to articulating in Spanish anything other than a mere formula for politeness in deference to your position. We have a langtong that's good for kindness, the ideal attitude of mind for prayer. The five parts of the prayer are *adoration*, which doesn't interest us; *supplication*, which doesn't interest us; *gratitude*, which doesn't interest us; *intercession*, which doesn't interest us; *confession*, which is the least interesting; and, finally, the only one to take into account today, *prostration*. I predict periods of renewed passion for explicitude (unfortunately for you, because where will we put the poison then?) These sentences, laden with ancient spasms, I read now with reproach, with fear of thinking that the langtong of national shame, once spoken, only remains to be grazed on by dust mites and, once excreted and expunged from the system, for the impossible allergies of women and men; but if man hasn't even been able to metabolize his own recently produced langtong, just imagine the nutrients he could still extract from the discard of dust mites. It's clear that reading doesn't necessarily extinguish what is written, but let's not let ourselves be blinded—oh, blindness would save so many good books—by the slackers. Did you believe that there was room in my existence for so many readers? No. This one for papa, this one for mama. I've said it before in a less evolved langtong: immutable dewlap of a pig, man, incapable of good; human gigot, meat salad. If you choose to write, you do it for people who aren't quite used to eating without a nosebag. I've done it and there are still linguatic hordes stuck in my throat because I don't have time or science for denouncing them all. Health, patience, and a gentle hand, that's how one day you'll see the gray hairs defeating the enemy.

You, my poison-taster, pretend not to mince words, as we say in Spanish, "not to have hairs on your tongue," but you do, fortunately: you have them very finely, super finely, just like intestinal villi. And if you rub one against another, you chirp like a cricket. Talk about mezzo-sopranoism! Sing, cricket, sing, syringe, syrinx! (That doesn't sound right to me, my jaw hurt. "My jaw hurt" doesn't sound right neither. I need to stop saying that; Spanish is not a monosyllabic langtong). Your answer to *Masterful*, in the end, was what has been said of all that is misunderstood: the hologram of a holocaust, the jedi sacrament, the momentary worship of what lasts an era, a jolt. I've already let on that the response from Obedience was positive, but what a revolting langtong Obedience used to express it! ... The plaudits were formulated with the same syllabary with which they had previously applauded the worst, the most pared down, between-season literature! The official cadaverists (because it is now well-known that the underground cadaverists are there just to dissent, to pretend to be subversive and, ultimately, to hit the mark with their judgments) said the same about my prickly prose as they said about the seamless prose of my peers, who seemed to be on summer vacation from language rather than writing. All's okay with everything's okay, but not all is okay in the same way, my friends. Faced with this state of affairs, my balloon was deflated but the color rushed to my cheeks, and I was convinced that I was indeed of this world, that I hadn't come here to fade but rather to pale just like everyone else in spite of my heavy status of hierarch (which weighs on me). I didn't expect Obedience to learn how to filter things, I figured Obedience already knew how to do it. The unanimity of Obedience, with unctuous hands, inserted the idea in my mind that there was no longer an inability to distinguish between wrought prose and wired prose, that neither inimical critics nor bardolators could differentiate the virulent epode from the barbituric caress.

They presented *Masterful*with the same face as the tamest
libel on the scene; they emphatically and emphysemically
equated *Masterful*and little books that could appeal ("tick-
le the palate") both to autumn-skilled young people as
to noxious octogenarians turning to literature for friend-
ship or whatever comes up. The difference had died, not
to mention the distinction. Criteria was as much at fault
as the opinion perpetrators themselves: we'd brought the
language down to zero, we'd turned the Spanish langtong
into something floppy and wimpy. They'd chosen me but
they could have chosen anyone. *Masterful*presided over a
Cretinocracy in full swing at who knows what infamous
preaperitif, but (what's worse) it was well-intentioned. If
my book ventured a little into the suspicious territory of
the incomparable, it went unnoticed by public opinion.

Let's be clear: no idea could be worse than leaving the
language in the hands of professionals. The anti-intellec-
tual pose, eager to shuffle the cards, pluck out a dirty card
and ask: "Was it this card? Was it this card? Answer me, yes
or no, that's all, YES or NO!"

The gentlest and most flattering thing that can be
said of Obedience is that Obedience was PRUDISH with
Masterful. And, after being prudish, Obedience was unanimous, as might be expected. A melé of caramels. *Masterful*,
despite being a Proteus with changing voice, remained unscathed in its gaseousness as the great chattering lords and
ladies of literature stressed its value. Life was a raffle. As
the langtong that was used to formulate the holy sanction
against *Masterful*was the same langtong that day in and day
out sanctioned the stercolaris prose of the moment —maybe they read *stercoralis*--, it stung my vanity. I set this face
you see now and held tight to my crown, telling myself that
this would pass. But it didn't pass. You can't keep speak-

ing according to certain things and then later according to other things. When a language serves to say one thing as well as its opposite with the exact same formulation, when ambitious expression is indistinguishable from commonplace, reform is imperative. The mini-magnum opuses that are fruits of this trend lead to our enemy, placidity, which is understandable. It's a simple thing, or do I just call it simple, so you won't realize yet that I'm going to explain it to you anyway, and it's not going to be pretty? It's not that I don't know how to explain myself better, it's really about who you are and that you don't deserve a better explanation. We'll get to know each other better soon. The *Masterful*libel was deactivated precisely because first some things were said, and then other things were said. Now we see that the work of fitting in is being done by others for you. I was hoping for what my mentor said, which was that "the title is already provoking scowls." (Despite the letter ñ[1], you have to admit the sentence is powerful.) Since my bravado was not particularly kind, you all felt the need to make it seem kind by softening it with your majordomo reading. Look, you have to be really twisted to make a rant seem like an excessively kind work! We have to recognize, for sure, that in this way you've managed to almost completely deactivate its meaning, and in celebration you toast with scowls. No! It's not fair to say that I'm good and to say that the guy next to me is good and to say that the guy next to him is good, because that's impossible or, at least, only a paratruth, because I don't see anyone beside me other than individuals afflicted by correctness, librettists deathly afraid of writing a verse that isn't instantly understood, copyists going crazy to avoid the slightest

---

[1] Translator's Note (TN): In the original, Giráldez quotes the preamble to Gracián's *El Criticón*: "el título está ya provocando zeño," hence the ñ, and which continues: "I hope that everything that is understood is assumed to be misunderstood."

16

wrinkle on the brow of their hypnotic god, the reader, the praegustator, their food-taster. Ultimately, that was what drove me to write a brief and ambitious libel, a torturous massage for about two hundred-odd people—how many more would you like to read you? you actually think they'll translate you, smarty-pants? The book hasn't been born yet that hurts a person who hasn't read it, at least not directly, and don't think I don't feel it. If only I could address you, the person who doesn't read, who will never get near my belches, and discover what you crave for fascination. We would have a good time, I promise you, I would promise you; we would be better friends than the reader and myself; I would provide you with everything you need, I would take care of you, I would look out for you. Because you, at least, have no qualms about what others believe moves you, your interest in redeeming yourself for the bad customs of your time, you are a human being with no intellectual shame, with the necessary and just modesty that God grants us in both manner and form. Now I let my body do what it wants, to lie in the pit of its desire, because people want what I want, and I have no problem with demanding tributes that even seem ridiculous to me, but this wasn't always the case.

The food-taster publicly demands brutal works; if you trusted what you hear, you'd believe he longed for the fire-eater's confession, that his character is so developed that it could deal with the fire-eater's confession. And then not. Then it turns out that what I was referring to was that you should stir up your feelings (not with these immaculate hands, please), that you should get emotional, and not that you should reveal the capital concerns of a civilization in order to relieve them with customized lies. It turns out my belches seduce the reader, the book and the editor, the scissors, stone and paper. The food-taster wants to be told a story, a manipulative fiction that puts a fist in the gut and aesthetic satisfaction in the lovaries. Perhaps there's no *epopoeia* in a discourse, in a written doctrine or in a homily? And if what one says isn't fiction, but rather the truth? Is a declaration less elevated than invention? An operetta should construct its langue and tongue attempting to resolve the discrepancies of language, and not be resigned to using the given language as an open-end wrench. To give birth to a super-language of words excited by artificial means—although whether dictates can be considered artificial means is not really clear. Why is aesthetic satisfaction bothersome, but not aesthetic revulsion? I'm afraid these voices still cry out for the Apollonian—when, at times, "A messy book may likewise hold much wisdom sound and terse"—and for domestication, and for suppression of variety, unaware that the wasting of nards, blood clots, handles and stacks of my libel were devised to serve as a sort of accessory frill. What the food-taster defends, given the excuse that his people want it this way and that it's a demand of his job as spokesperson, is wholehearted sameness, tautologies, gargantruism and a familiar melody. If what you were asking for was fascination, I could respect that, but let's be serious, I'm fed up with your epiphanies: what you want, food-taster, is a vehicle for prudence, not a principle of cruelty and two stomach cramps. A communication—the cricket sings—but an instantaneous communication and one without interference or dissonance: a colony made of holy water, that's what you want. Verbal practices distanced from what's practical and beyond a prophetic or fanatic function are inconvenient for you. But essentially, we want both parts to be the same, my friends: a message by langtong, what else?

We've crossed paths at a thousand parties. I see you coming: I can tell you're furious because of your lumbar arch, prominent from refraining from insults, but I can't refrain from respiration. The food-taster and I are used to finding ourselves at opposite ends of the whip, from where he hollowly asks me for a "cierta ferocidad técnica." He gets it. I give it to him. Bam. I tell them all: Look into the depths of this urinal: here is where the magic happens. In the years of passion for explicit things, from which, despite everything, I've emerged, I give you what your loved ones desire, what they believe they desire. I give my permission for publication of *Masterful*, oh! not so much a libel as balm of Fierabrás! It's fair to wonder when the reluctant public became this fighting cock, this belligerent ego, when it studied with such rigor for a shadow play monologue. The food-taster is he who waits for others to fall quiet in order to speak out, the most polite, unequaled, the son of the son of the son of the son of the sword swallower, who knows more than his father, the steel and the throats about how to do what he does, and he explains it to you super-pre-recorded, too bad it's so pre-recorded, how the thunder dances when the lightning no longer shines its light, eh? It won't be me who says it's *ridículo*, because even the thunder has a right to comment, of course, but to deny that the lightning came first would be foolish.

I've often told myself that it would have been better for me to write a lesser work, period—as I was also advised by my own sanity, the nextvicepremier, my valet, the parish of the entire Mother Mimicry, for lack of a better word, the convulsionettes and my enemies— at least, in this way, I'd have a little bit of idiocy potion leftover in the hollow of my backbone because now my marrow is only good for making stew and not much more than that. So many

voices, one has access to so much good advice… I certainly
wouldn't eat any of those tongues even if they were boiled
in blissful juice; I'd sooner eat—as I've already eaten—my
own writing utensils. Thanks to the Peace, I've been able
to clearly reconstruct my genesis, I've been able to see the
Creator teaching his assistants, offering them the dummy
of my body and saying: "All it needs is the topping, what
will you put on this one?" And those playful elves, without
whose assistance the Supreme Maker would snip off my
balls, surrounded my incomplete figure and jabbed their
little sticks into the colorful sockets and gave me an extra
dose of pride. May this avuncular and digressive comic
strip serve no purpose and provide no excuse for me! My
contemporaries and I were the least little problem in literature in order to become the greatest problem in language.
The only thing this State can't tolerate is argumentative
disobedience and believe me when I say that my people
are doing all that's within our power to study the possibility of varying my judgment in this respect. Nothing would
please us more, in fact, with a hand to your heart, than to
tolerate a bit of disobedience, but, between us, who would
emerge most compromised? Without unanimity, there is
no possible democracy, that's clear. It might seem cata-
strophic, but undoubtedly unanimity has succeeded, and
the "cans," and the "maybes," are resources for cutting-
to-the-quick to attract you to the bunker for thy own good.
The thing is that judgment and opinions have little to do
with unanimity, despite how contradictory that might seem
to us; they pertain to different planes of reality. That's why,
when I speak of unanimity, I'm not including the readers
among my stats, just the others, those who make up …
well, there's no other way to say it: unanimity. I won't be
so rude as to try to include my subjects in a category I

already know would cause them a frontal and even lateral repulsion. Unanimity considered me a gentleman, a master Mastuerzo, when I was none other—poor little me—than a ubiquitous fava bean cook, the same here as there, the same whether protected by a casemate or an aduar (see how I even know how to name petty objects?) I dressed the saints, albeit not in compliance, but rather enraged. To the point that I have a message for the convulsionettes' princes who have so lauded me, and that is that all my serum, all the serum they've been swallowing so eagerly for all these years, are caramels and will destroy them from inside when they recrystallize. Don't let yourself get cold, don't let yourself stop moving, don't stop rubbing yourself, don't stop. Now, after dedicating myself to telling you all about myself from A to Y, I know I've done poorly by using Spanish. Although well-regarded, it's not important, because friends and enemies will all meet at the end of the road, where you'll devour my tail with salsa Cholula.

What do you think? All told, your stomach was the customs port for the debut of *Masterful*. Faith in the evaluation of all values implies the advent of a coherent champion critic, the *lumen de lumine*, so saintly as to be almost inexistent. Unfortunately, we reached the point where a person is either a critic or a reader, but never the two at once. Anyone who automatically elevates *Masterful* to the category of the Vulgate is just as mistaken as anyone who devalues it, but they are just as mistaken if they compare it with anything other than *Masterful*, such that both the consenting judges and those bucking back act with equal sophistry: all of them, absolutely all of them, are mutes and muzzles. My clappers and lappers are responsible for my deification, the heights of my gibberish are directly under their influence. You'll have noticed that when I speak of defects, I use the plural and when I enumerate virtues, I employ the singular: this has to do more with honesty than presumptuousness. I don't need to be presumptuous because Obedience, mistress of past and future cadavers, assumed nearly conjugal postures with me thanks to my many offerings, so aroused in the face of my vehemence. With such a dirty tongue, if the critics have a dog—yes, just one dog, it's well known that all the critics in Spain live in the same house and eat at the same table, and I'm not referring to whoever gives them sustenance but rather to their coordinates—it's very probable that they call it Kubla. When the critics write to me (he or she or they would have to rinse his or her or their hands with alcohol before writing me, and then write to me) to tell me they're reading *Masterful*, I know they're not reading *Masterful*; I'm firmly convinced they're not reading *Masterful*. When journalists write to me to tell me they're reading *Masterful* and that they think it's fabulous, I know they aren't reading *Masterful* and they don't think anything about it; that at most they've touched the book to convince themselves that their intention authorizes them to call me and speak to me as if they'd already read it and, in the end: I've heard a lot about your operetta and I'll read it in no time, but not yet, not today, not in your lifetime. The fact that vehemence subdues whoever goes around looking for style shouldn't surprise anyone. It's said that *Masterful* inspired silence, but without specifying who muted the voices. There were geniuses before my book ever saw the light and it extinguished the light or it made you think it had extinguished it. Due to a bad reading habit, I was counting on the *plácet* of fortuitous judgment, and then, opinion tilted and its dogs surrounded me after superficial scrutiny (as well as brief scrutiny). So, it could be said that the opinion of the bardolators has condemned me to self-assurance, thanks to the word-kissers. They made me intelligent in their minds and almost convinced me that in fact I really was. I was one thimble away from believing it. At the book presentations everybody bought *Masterful*, they started to read it right then and there and they couldn't stop the nosebleeds—okay, if I'm exaggerating, stop me with a kiss, because I no longer understand any other language and least of all your Spanish—until they reached the last page. (I'm exaggerating again, sure: how's a Spanish reader going to know what to do on the last page of a book, if it's something they've never seen before in their entire life? They would confuse it with a tuba or a syringe filled with silicone.) It might look like I'm dramatizing, but nothing could be further from my nature than to present the facts differently than they could be said to have happened. Be that as it may, those who believed they were carrying the Ark of the Covenant on their shoulders were really carrying my coffin aloft; they believed they were bearing the diseased literature of a diseased Virgil, but it was me pretending to be dead and writing with a raised hand. And I dared do it in this way because the idea that someone was writing honestly didn't seem serious to me; my millennium and aristocratic education (that is: the one I'd given myself) didn't prevent me from seeing that clarity was prohibited and that what was triumphing was a postcard esotericism of sorts. I'm a cultivator and I store my venom in my codex, but a writer of race doesn't exist because stupidity is not a race, it's a condition. And that's how my day would go, between doing kingly things, convulsioning and virulence; convulsioning, virulence and doing kingly things, and once in a while a bit of doodling. How long has it been since I lost that sensation of "I read at night and become strong and I will overcome you all, you bunch of slackers?" The duties of my post, the attributes of the crown, the paternal obligations, tourism among family members, the privileges that end up becoming punishment: everything holds me back now and it's been so long since I practiced self-improvement during the night. There was nothing behind my great shield, not a single idea; I lived in an inertia of enablement of poise and faith in myself. And this could be seen by my enemies, my admirers and those who decide who goes and who remains. And those who remain tend to be the most inoffensive (on the condition that they don't appear that way). Now that I'm sure of it, I can tell you we gave you cat-and-rabbit poison.

Look at yourself, my dear food-taster, you smile as if you had one last ace up your sleeve, which is why I like you, because you need help but won't accept it, though it's at your service, unlike a bardolator, who asks for help just to draw you in and then to shake your hand with a spongy grip and (who knows?) perhaps drenched in vinegar. You both need, you know this, a new predicator to govern you with a gentle hand; the gentle hand, a rotten pepper hand, a mallet that, when it falls full force on your loved ones, has the advantage of not breaking, nor will it break anything or leave a mark. If you hit yourself, it's probably against someone else's head, but you can't blame the pepper hand, because take a look at this hand, for f's sake, peppers don't have knuckles, my friend. Who am I to be you? says the pepper hand. But I was telling you that the bardolator, prince of convulsionettes, is a farcical job in life, which is not the same as that of the reader, since such repugnance is rarely feigned. And they also have in common (why not top it off?) the digestive system of a bat, which shits what it eats almost before sinking its teeth into it. Besides their certain degree of cleverness, they variously compose—the bardolators and enemies—a unanimous Obedience, an Obedience that governs, the same Obedience that gave the designation of artefact, *sataniquissimo*, *pasquino* and other things, to the treatise I have entitled, with scarce modesty, *Masterful*: a failed and repugnant operetta, pure blablaing, if you will, but still an operetta in the end; and the reader, at the very least, has the responsibility, in my opinion, to identify the fictitious caca, for which God has provided him the stomach of a worm as I've provided you all with a healthy government and a First-World sewage system. There, I suggested that if you give up on the first page, you're no good to me either as a reader or an enemy; what do you want, representation or vision? Because I offer you vision, and I've already told you I don't know how to do anything else. To be sincere with you, I don't know how to tell a story, what I do is more like elaborating comments on the vague limit between a problem and a solution. Being terrible has not demanded much effort for me, in general (my lineage has probably smoothed the way for me, I wouldn't deny it), and as far as being an *enfant*, that passed me by before I knew I had an appetite for publishing and resolving, therefore, to pretend that was to be my life. In my view, there is more salvation in one thing than the other (I'm referring to representation and vision). What do you want? I got distracted and no one—clumsy from deafness—responds? The fact is I was born with the curse of an unshakeable faith in myself or, much the same thing, I was born with adolescence. The formulas of modesty were going bad on me through disuse, they formed obstructions, thrombosis, ingurgitations, *tutti obstats*, lumps that couldn't find a way out. There's a kind of modesty that began to take hold among writers of the generation before me and that I consider intolerable, by which I mean the sincere, real type. Why write if you don't believe you're a genius? If you don't believe you're the best, don't waste my time. Don't ask me for anything if, in the end, you're going to ask for it as a favor. The Spanish operetta, they would say! Herein lies the desire for style. What you all call "Spanish"; I still haven't given it a name. In the Spanish operetta there is no comment with hemlock, but rather an inverted cross, inverted, an inverted Coco Chanel symbol, gentlemen with their hands extended who ask you, "which way to my tomb?," clammed-up breadwinners and the occasional fucking jeweler consuming their own lymphocytes, Spaniards who chatter "take care of your money, it's the nicest thing you've got," worthy scribes who community members encourage every time they finish a sentence by yelling PARKLIFE!, posing on their bums in high relief, now believing themselves to be fakirs; in Spanish literature there are a thousand ball-swallowers for every sword-swallower.

There's no telling where to begin killing today's Spanish writer. You really have to have courage to write in the crude langtong you think in, and if you think in the langtong used by the national news broadcasters, perhaps it's better to waste your time in very different kinds of time-wasters. The least we can ask of us bad writers, Spanish writers, is that we shouldn't write nonsense, that we know enough to limit ourselves so that some semi-form liposurges from the mass: that we write, instead of probing (give the probes to your father, please). We bad writers, Spanish writers, could be recognized by our fondness for the verb *armar*, by our interminable lists of acknowledgements, because we confuse *óbolo* with *óbice* and *óbice* with *óvido*, which is all the same: because we aren't clear on the elementary signs of signation which we've chosen for excretion.[2] Because, apparently, we make use of other people's time and not—like all other mortals—exclusively of our own time. Someone had to stand up as a motivator, an artificial priest, but I've already said I look down on you as much as on anyone. I was thinking my libel should stop being my protégé: I have to learn to let it play with the wolves—I told myself—that someone would even know how to suckle it better than me. And I sinned out of goodness. I didn't know how to situate myself in the shadowy place-home of the other, because the other didn't exist. Modern novelists, the last ones to escape unscathed from using that label, dedicated themselves to sauerkrauting their writing during the decade immediately before *Masterful*. I shut them up and you gushed your gratitude. I can't complain. But that was your duty. I'm not going to feign an appetite for offending you at every opportunity, I'll say it clearly: all artists, of low and high birth, have made bad jokes of you and they've done it with class. I won't be guilty of feeding the conscience of the species ambiguously. I'm tired of writers with the reputations of nuns repeating old jokes with no new sense of humor. Here you have my grain of truth: writers, writer, writers who have opened the Spanish mouth again during my absence are sleeping guards, life is paralyzed in the prose of their vulgar narratives of heart-stopping style, style that deserves no analysis or appraisal. Shitmouths with felonious attitudes, bread and circus performers. You think I can't put myself in the place of the downtrodden? But I have no ground beneath me! I could be the king of spades. Yes, someone has to tell you that for some years the world has been doomed to end in frivolous black masses. And then I arrived, whether

---

[2] TN: Here, we lose the recurring play on words in Spanish between excogido/escogido, escretar/excretar, excribir/escribir… oh, well.

summoned by friends or enemies of the langtong, I don't know. Something isn't working when you go from taking communion freely to doing it by drawing lots. In general, nobody knows where you came from, and everyone dares to speculate about how you got inside. No one speculates about what "inside" means, so the reception aesthetic has been reduced to just that: the work of a chamberlain. Despite all that, they accepted me, who knows why. When *Masterful*came out, the last writers muttered things about their intentions to improve without any real guarantees, and we well know promises are made to one and all, even to horses, of course. The same writers who saluted my first publication met their ends even as they wrote the last thing they were ever going to write: that salute. I have to admit that a salute that contains its own conclusion has a nearly supreme elegance that goes right to my head and deserves major kudos; I have always kept it in mind since then whenever I've felt compelled to write attacks and denunciations of bardolotry. The few writers who succeeded me were not exactly my epigones but rather my clownettes. You incapable writers of your own intimate ideas, sybarites of failure, waiting to be pollinized, so receptive without realizing that your entire attitude drives the contraception of any possibility for art. You are all too open, surely you have a kind of faith that something fertilizes the excrement you leave here and there, protected at times by the previous dejection of some other author—about your dejection, I can't deny that you are indeed the authors, of course, you are, and among the best, you get the prize for best *creator*! Good operettas hide the degree to which they are pleasing just as well as the bad ones, they affect a certain acquired theatrical detachment, which Obedience does not forgive in the master felon. After assuming my failure, I wouldn't have had enough feet to flee on, if I hadn't realized how easy it was to supplant genius, or at least save it a warm seat beside me. Bad writers show the same profession of faith in themselves as a soft cock; I at least kept it hard, a narcissus in flower. Mine was *farro*, it's true, but everyone else's was automatic farro of the worst kind, bran, instead of the nectar that some people declared they got out of *Masterful*. Was I an answer or an *Anser anser* (in Latin), a giant duck, a goose without bump? Maybe not, but I was convinced I was—unlike them—distilled, a quintessential brandy of anarchy; and you come here refluxing porridge and sipping controlled milk, showing off virtues of demogreasy, politiquevérité. You detonated salvific salvas for vacuous authors and the atmosphere reeked of singed hair or death, depending on whether you incinerated more or less bald corpses. Today, however, the flabby points of the shanty I've called *Masterful* are clear for me, and I tend to agree more with my few detractors than with my bootlicking claque. You are probably aware that I owe all my privileges and a large part of my financial records to the publication of *Masterful* (the Crown was able to award me the right to be respected, but only *Masterful* rendered me deserving of my enemies), that infamous *cum grano salis solaris*, novice and nonetheless unfortunately elevated to the category of nuclear by those who held the power to tighten the skins of the period. And I've also already made it clear that, at an evil hour, Unanimity handed me the keys to its hole and that, from then on, everything was going in and out through the tunnels.

Bla.

But let's be frank: *Masterful* never hurt a dahlia, take it from me. I confess that *Masterful* didn't say anything, but the applause drowned out any kind of reflective operation.

An imitation of the sepsis itself in Gracián's forgotten lang-tong; prosody turned inside out; various levels of difficulty, like in a frigging game room; solvable puzzles that didn't matter in the least if they were solved; invisible and unsatisfying challenges and super obvious erudite landing strips whose surfacery required an awesome and infinite lack of inspiration. Too many clues planted along the road toward honest obtuseness. Aberrant name-dropping. A lot of manipulation, blatant rubbing against your master's leg and metaphors created in the spirit of packaging. The perfect space for the press to insert the word "unclassifiable" as if it were a bedpan. (One editor even went so far as to tell me to forget about calling it *Regüeldo*[3] because of the diaeresis over the u and that it's been proven to be impossible to establish the diaeresis in the orthographic national imaginary: which would make the operetta invisible in the bookstores.) The misadventures of *Masterful* are clunky and hold little interest for me, even less than autobiographical narration, so disdained these days, which is why I let it loose in the middle of this place like a laying hen. I suspect that narratives that do without "a plot of misadventures" and trust in large part to the power of the written word are really being written for friends, that is to say: for those of you who don't read us. That's why they're written in really loud voices. For the enemy, for those who read us, we have to create "tangible" characters, to describe spaces as if for someone who has never gone out in the open, to advance the anecdote just like in life: through action. I was interested in processes—today, just those that lead to the executioner of peace, who is focused on bestowing sorrow on confessed bardolators or those betrayed by their families (the figure of the liberated

---

[3] TN: There is no unanimity concerning the etymology of the word "regüeldo" (belch) and its virtues, except in one respect: the two dots above the u represent gases in suspension.

bardolator is another song, and I've already said that for me the ability to sing has been denied): the sermon of the processus, not its execution, the instant in which all meaning is atomized… Well, that which you, my dear food-taster, confuse with execution (just so we understand each other).

My demoiselle told me I've put all the collocations upside down. Silly was anyone who was not me, blind anyone who could not see me. Today I disagree: in *Masterful*, there are too many meanderings, menanderings and leanderings; too much serum of repurposed truth. Humor completely truncated. Bad, all bad. A lot of movement where I only wanted to create a *tableau* vivant (only for the pleasure of doing something French for a change), the death rattles of an almost still life, the ultimate fart of M. Valdemar. And, furthermore, you'd say, an argument can't be an operetta, a voice can't be a character, and I'd tell you: is there anything more puerile than needing a character like a piece of bread for pushing your food? You couldn't get yourself to believe in the corporeality of the characters, their reality; and I'm not surprised: the main character was more like a gas than an entity. It's revealing that you're always looking for new voices, but you don't want to hear the speech of a single voice; what you'd like, I deduce, are voices that await you outside rather than inside of books… What are you afraid of? Don't be so suspicious, so what if the voices go more where they're permitted than where one secretly would like them to go? Nobody's going to judge you, the voices penetrate you like mouthwash, like a prodigious chip, like the lukewarm miso soup they pour into Hamlet's father's ear, internally connected to the British Mouth, to sit there and, as we well know: to cause an ear infection, an infection of speech. But what can I convince you of, right? You can't write by genuflecting, nor by puffing out your cheeks, and for finding a middle ground we have publishers, agencies and special awards. There was a publishing house, Jekyll & Jill, who published Magistral in the past, and there's another publishing house, Malas Tierras, who asked me to translate *Notable American Women* by Ben Marcus (but that's something I'm still not sure I'm going to tell you about). What else was there in *Masterful*, good or bad? Too much of everything, too much time for isolation and not even a lousy tube of Vaseline; nothing and nothing that starts in *Masterful* is ever finished, which I can acknowledge now, with relief. And then there was the format of the book, purist and prohibitive, with tremendous pros, such as its stunning color, and very comprehensible cons, such as its rebellious bent; some elements of the book said *drink me, eat me,* and others said *don't buy me.* Perhaps, the last one—without losing sight of the infectious nature of my text—made *Masterful* the best camouflaged banal operetta of its genre. In this respect, it met the same fate as other banal operettas: printed on paper and celebrated on paper. The other type of operetta, the type of truly grand operetta, tends to be celebrated in silence, asymmetrically and without unanimity. I didn't want to write an operetta that was correct but rather a sacramental demolition derby. To produce a piece with nutritional value, you have to be prepared to be perceived as problematic. Confession of faith, whether mistaken or not, is always problematic, and my faith, as previously mentioned, was in myself. The unusual proportions of affectation that autobiography favors led me to discover my ugly innovative technique. Literature has nothing to do with life, forget that idea: literature and life are two entities that don't coincide on any reality plane; and, yet literature only exists in terms of autobiography. Since logic didn't dictate anything and I'd stopped putting my talents at the service of ideas, I had no other choice but to abide by the rules of language.

Narcissism and the false credo declared by Unanimity took care of the rest.

In Spain you can't write the first sentence of *Masterful*, which I won't reproduce now because why on earth let them eat bread, but, yes, you can write things like "I stare at *my own* hands"[4] and get compliments the next day. And no one is going to wonder in whose mouth this one or that one passed the night. Spain is magic, and the criteria in all areas is merely superstition, old people's stuff. It's Eden, Bruges-la-Morte *à rebours*; Spain, a smear of rouge. The secrets of the scribe during our century are provided to be deciphered in *Masterful*; what can't be understood, even by myself, I hid behind an attempt to balance a horseshoe-like moustache on my upper lip. There were some who truly liked it and some who fibbed about liking it, my little libel. The others are adornment, in reduced and anomalous numbers, among the files of offended readers; the others wanted something different and they bought something different from what they really wanted: I understand very well the sense of anxiety and anger of these poison-tasters, because the same thing happens to me with respect to them. Whoever saw nothing more than a pretext for energizing my turbine in the structure of my libelous book was probably right; at least, that's what I think now. Outright Obedience, in the face of that turbulent festival of slander and flattery, created a decisive slattery (it couldn't be any other way). They eat my *melos* to the marrow. The large operettas (have you ever imagined that the size of ambition had anything to do, at times, with the size of talent?) have chamberlains who are too rigorous, hardly masters of their words, occasional misanthropes—it's already

---

[4] TN: Semantic calque in Spanish: "Me miro mis manos".

clear that large operettas choose their readers poorly—poor dancers and poor drinkers, lacking nonchalance and complaining of hoarse throats. Brilliant work? That's what the poison-taster is for, not to say that he's read it but to prophesize about it. Every half lustrum a fool in a big way, a fool fully equipped, with all the perks, with Ariadne and Arachne's thread, a fool who is probably writing the Far Too Kind Operetta, the fool rises up and announces that the operetta is dying. He'd be speaking about his home. In my home, the operetta was alive and well and there was no place for the cowardly idea that everything had already been written and there's nothing new under the sun. We must be sunbathing under different suns, I'm afraid. At least, that's what I was thinking. Genuine literature, or what is the same thing: non-Spanish literature, doesn't announce its plans; non-Spanish literature has to remain quiet so as not to interrupt the buffoonery; non-Spanish literature is less rebellious and dissident than it thinks it is, it's not so young anymore. Nonetheless, whoever says no one in this world is capable of writing something good anymore, only believes that because he lacks the talent to even imagine what his neighbor would do with half his talent. Doomster Spanish writers, living porky pies, the intestinal flute plays with so much flattulery as your cheeks might contain and you make such a face! Your face squinches up like donkey veins and you forget there's another class of person on the other side of your stench, that not everyone prostrates themselves before your Obedience and your dear fucking kids in Spain, the tomb of copyrights, but more to the point, why does this papal nuncio, who no one listens to or hears today the way they should, why does he deny this if not because his ancestors were broken? To the writer who thinks that nothing new can be done: may he never make us read anything by him. Kindness is the enemy of the new. The great author in our times of the Far Too Kind Operetta believes he is the grand prescriber but is no more than a Chinese fortune cookie. There's no danger of offending him because there's no possibility of his reading as far as this line; he's a person only concerned with his own marital gains. They'll go on handing out prizes and penalties of identical value to those who'll accept them. Courtesy is a conditioned reflex, and the reader is someone who has learned to rid himself of that fault. If a genius wants to act in such a way and not fall into ruin, he'll have to find a balance between not going hoarse from sucking cocks and trusting publication of his material to crummy chance. I've lost the joy of genius and now I'll lose the joy of buffoonery. That's how things are, so it's understandable that the idea of linguistic pillaging didn't seem so outlandish from a distance. Is there a different name for the chamberlain who stands at the door and another for the one who announces the people as they enter, a master of halls and avant-halls? Or are they simply sentries? Are they mine or Marcus's? I believe it's possible for a really smart person to write a bad book and I also believe that a fool has the ability to produce a brutal book, truly savage; whoever thinks differently doesn't know squat about the publishing business. I believe in chance and lineage (the first doesn't need the second, but the second needs the first). You only need old money, family money. And then there's only the other. You only have to be capable, gifted, touched, crazy for good, and alone, very alone. Alone in your intent and your ambition, which would be on a par with what was described by Volodine, Kronauer, Draeger and Lutz, when wondering about their own work, as "Writing in a foreign language as if writing in French."

So, I stopped reading Spanish writers because I was constructing a language and, in books that weren't mine, the language I encountered was already made. Few poison-tasters were able to filter out such perversity, few could see in me not only the importer but also the exporter of shame. However, neither polemicists nor polysemistes knew how to bring me down from the little inferno with a podium I'd mounted. It was all laughter and no reprobation, just more laughs and, as I say: no reprobation, just laughs; all the way to periodontitis! and still no reprobation. The deal is, I would have preferred that they halt me, that they chide me for the superlushness of my uneven houri prose; that the poison-taster, the crestfallen impaler, the trembling impersonator of *esperpento*, of the grotesque, of beauty, would say to me: Abandon all form, show some respect for the monotony of life, it's okay, it would appear they've ordained you to the Carthusian order after who knows how many years of disordered habits and you still don't even know how to do that well; with all that we've given you, all that we've read to you, so much training in buffalo milk and look, no: you like to write weird stuff? Very well: let's talk weird. You do whatever appeals to you, but the illusion of instantaneous legibility is the law for these sauces. You claim: I don't feel like speaking like you. And the critics reply: Sure, but then you won't want comprehensible awards, we'll give you awards in line with your diction. The deal is that we overestimate reader comprehension (which has no relevance at all) and for that reason we also overestimate reader incomprehension, which is inherent to the prefix particle *in-*: "lack of." You've confused talent with Poise, the ability to write and have free time, you've confused a great lack of talent with genuine talent, and Poise ends up leading us to boldness, contempt, perfectionism. When you hear me speak in an accessible tone, it'll be because you have access to your own martyrdom, because I'm accessible, but not foolish or didactic, and the only thing I let you access easily is my vessel of fury: I'm only concerned with sprinkling this ground with astonishment. Don't write: SPEAK. What I'm speaking to you about is this, in the end: if you don't know how to pronounce it, you don't know how to do it. If you don't know how to say "colonoscopy" it's very likely you shouldn't practice it, except passively. A person is who they are when they write: if you describe violent orgies, even though you don't actually do them, you have what it takes for bacchanalia. If you know how to make water, you also know how to sip water and you know how to say: what a ton of notable American women we have here tonight, reading Marcus's book.

Ben Marcus could be speaking to you here and now, dear august prescriber, and not me, if we were all committed to the prudent commitment of abandoning the Spanish langtong. Ben Marcus could have happened to Spain if it still had a langtong. If only my eyes had forever ignored the achievement of the blessed North American Mouth of Ben Marcus carried to its completion! Cursed be the day that he finished writing his concubine words about others and declared his scathing critique of them complete, and also of his replacement, me. I don't have a natural skill for tolerating a lack of ambition, I insist, but I liked the world more when I was convinced that I was the cause of the wasteland it had become, where the ambition of men was just a memory. I still have time to be exempted from becoming a beloved person, highly regarded by my dear fools, and to become a perfect companion, a perfect Marcus flunky as the words danced so well in the ether of my mouth when I was so full of myself, and now I'm unable to hear anything other than a magical bellowing every time I speak, a frigging Wunderhorn turnip. Now I see that the novelty of my libel—ay, not so much a libel as Fierabrás' balm! —consists in the fact that, for the first time, the writing of an animal has been printed in a mollycoddled rustic edition. And it turns out the animal was playing the harmonium. My genius was not genius but rather peculiarity, eccentricity. And they all danced. And I thought they would dance still more, over time. But no. I'm the emperor's new suit. The leporello suit of a king, invisible to reasonable people. The leporello suit, invisible to reasonable people, of a king, to be more specific; the king plays a plastic melodica in this sentence just as he came into this world: simple, naked and deified. The poise with which I rose to fame was alarming for me, rather than calming. Why I was comfortable listening to people whose opinions deserved none of my respect is something I haven't bothered to explain to myself until now. During the short time that my post lasted, my subject was the ruined intellect of my century, and isn't it suspicious that the riff-raff composed of our most distinguished comrades in imbecility, whom I've shaken my fist at so many times, should accept my high-octane insults without shielding themselves in any way? For this very reason, no one can shame or blame me for my conduct if, tonight, I choose to remain in the comfort of these maws.

The time may have come for us to punch a hole in the beauty of the Spanish langtong and shit worms in it until it's full. Today, Spanish is a cretin langtong. Evidently, French and Portuguese and Catalan, by proximity, must find themselves in a similar state of decadence; German has always given me calluses; the British Mouth is too narrow for my head. Why not kiss the North American Mouth and rip out its tongue? But to be sure: only the best North American mouths. Where is excellence to be found? So, I've reached this point and, again: until recently, you were longing for a sensible project and you found pleasure by joining with Obedience. I'd have to say, in your favor, I never told you or enlightened you about the method I proposed for kidnapping an entire langtong and carrying it away with me.

So, I was to be the translator?[5]

As you know, before joining up with Burroughs on the obvious idea of language as a virus, Marcus wrote a false and extreme memorandum under the title, *Notable American Women*. Getting away with it is as hard as getting past it. But what if *Notable American Women* were a booby-trap-country, a garden-city of tortures, a disgusting porno planet in a planisphere?

Was I to be the translator?

The most malevolent elements of Obedience can guarantee that I entered *Notable American Women* seeking refuge but in fact I came to the point of wanting to poison it. These are not adumbrations; this is the truth: I went to Marcus to procure a langtong but Marcus won't let me get away with it. Always keep your tongue in your mouth, he says, and don't speak with your mouth open, he says. So, I'm trying to decide what command to give you all: a) *Be snake apprentices*, or else b) *Convert to Marcus*. Should I let you go on making tacky sacrifices to *Masterful* and resign myself to my confinement or should I begin the work of an apostle and force this mouth open? Vanity is no longer my most distinctive feature—the positive judgment of your honorable Obedience is something I've overcome the

---

5 TN: The more, the merrier.

way one overcomes a fever—but prudence certainly is. I was not the motordivinity I thought I was. I'm indebted to my pubis. The bardolators probably wouldn't want to find out I'm a fraud, that I have secretly been deposed and now I should share a similar fate to theirs, but there is someone who does indeed have an obligation to know full well what they're eating, and that's why I've called you. The poison-taster only has two obligations: swallowing and not being immortal or immune to poison. On the other hand, why would you trust my judgment when it comes to the North American Mouth since I've shown no signs of discretion or restraint or moderation towards containing my success? You'll tell me. And me: am I the enemy of whoever surpasses my talent, or do I have to devote my energies to putting them in circulation? For now, let's not discuss the greater or lesser happiness of this reflection, of the reflection with which Ben Marcus's book begins, my new master or my prison of love or nothingness, this shall be seen when my secretaries decide on a less sunny day whether all of this is something I'm saying or just keeping quiet. You'll be wondering what other things my people do to entertain themselves—my secretaries, bardolators and poison-tasters don't cease to be men and women of the Crown, after all: I've sent them to beat hell out of the Mediterranean. They won't come back until they really punish it, and meanwhile no one will notice if I'm in charge or not (the difference is so minimal). If there's one thing Marcus has taught me deep in my bones, it's that I DON'T MATTER anymore, that the vain word has come to an end; that, since we're together, I no longer exist. That book, if it ever sees the light, consumes the light and saves you from seeing your own faces as they truly are. Forget about the mental thing, about oxen seminating black semen in white pages: with

Notable American Women, Ben Marcus tells us what's left to write—have you had the opportunity to taste something so perverse and refined in all your years of office?—and his word is *turbamulta*, and his word confiscates what interests no one for his own benefit, and his word is revealing, and his word is enough. But all we human beings are identical. Any human being forced to choose between proselytism and silencing their genius would choose the same position: whichever is most appropriate to their character: silencing if it conforms to them—their character, I mean—and proselytism if, as in my case, they're tired of exerting that contrite passion that we generally identify with personality itself. And there'll be those who revile that pusillanimity, of course, it's clear there also has to be a place for poison in this world, and people are just as safe to serve as receptacles as the best vials.

I don't want to be the translator.[6]

(1) Dictates are real, and they are articulated in (2) a superlanguage that (3) we mortals can only translate into languagio, each according to their own abilities. To call (1), (2) and (3) "inspiration" is not to understand anything, unless, of course, we're discussing inhalation.

I'm a fraud and a refugee (this latter only per sonority, I admit). I see it clearly now. Understand me well (a manner of speaking, you'll never know anything about this if I decide not to give you a taste of Marcus's own words, but who knows? Tonight, I could still write to Guillermo and Nico, the publishers at Malas Tierras, and tell them I won't be able to translate *Notable American Women*, but I'd lose the opportunity to lose the original forever), I still haven't overcome my own vanity. For deification purposes, I've already prepared the speech I'd bestow upon your minds, the grandstands and bilges, on the day of my official recogni-

---

[6] TN: It's OK to cut off your nose to spite your face.

tion: Grandstands and balconies of Your Honorable Obedience, no one comes to mind who has invented anything worthwhile, essentially, either in this century or any of the previous centuries, and literature is no exception. The cure? I don't think I have to express much gratitude: more than once, it has saved Auster or Hesse, almost senselessly, from what is really useful for History, with sublime disdain for natural selection, and it would continue curing dispensable scribes if *Masterful* hadn't exterminated every last one of the eggs or sperms with a bent for written digression. If I have to choose a human invention that seems valid to me, the only thing that occurs to me is the shoehorn. The shoehorn really serves a purpose, and every home should have at least one if they want to be considered civilized homes.

Basically, before I'd read Marcus's book, I lived by taking refuge in a modest dialectic, waiting for a highly probable—what can I say, my mind was living in my head and didn't know anything else, poor thing—glorification, counting the points on my crown to pass the time. I'm confident this doesn't seem incomprehensible to you: the intimate conviction of being insuperable diminishes the importance of the kindness of the real opinions one harvests or that you decide to support. Knowing that one can eliminate anyone by means of three words, four at the most, one sleeps peacefully, a peace that you the subjects will never know, you the dominated, the still unpoisoned ones, the insecure ones, apprentices of vanity but with little dedication, which I will never know again after having bumped into the book that rattled me in every sense, in my own head, me, playing in my own house, just imagine! In light of the North American Mouth, *Masterful*, the space that the invention of *Masterful* was occupying in my brain, was smooshed, to say it in a word that is smooshed just attempting to fulfill its own meaning. The pain was less dramatic than the humiliation, and the humiliation was almost fun if compared to the panic. A few hours before, my decisions—I believed—were the law for the world and caused the perception of History as we know it, in one sense or another, to oscillate. At first, I succeeded in persuading myself that my writing represented the unknown zenith of this era and no other literary quality existed that even had the curiosity of disputing this place with me, because the super-personal space of the prose of those writers speaking to you would not allow for another style in comparison without hurting them, I told myself; and if that sounds ridiculous, it's because during that period, I was not dictated by the North American Mouth, or because you were reading me wrong and everything sounded stupid when read by you alone (boop-boop-a-doop). If you don't understand me, it's probably because you've installed AdBlock. If I were to muffle Ben Marcus's novel, if I were to hide it from you all! But I've come to an end here, considering whether to undertake an apology for what the North American Mouth set out as bait for me. Dead bait that witnesses all of this through a pacification of the senses that one should experience when acquiring the absolute sense of certainty that it's impossible to resuscitate. Why is it so hard to believe that Ben Marcus is alive if he doesn't live to redeem himself, nor that he exists merely as bait for a megalomaniac Spaniard who can't stop talking? This is what it's like to be dead, as I understand it: the extinction of all impatience. Is it only Marcus who can play at this, the stealing of genius, the omission of genius? His genius, in some way, is the absence of vanity as a fruit of extreme lucidity which has enabled him to understand that he is no more the *artifex* of his work than his langtong is.

I should be translating Stephen Fry; he actually pays the bills.

But what kind of innocent world is this in which God wakes up one day and He's no longer anybody? The king has become a Paragon! I hate myself for knowing it. How have I been able to enjoy *Notable American Women* to the point of no longer devouring your vocation as a reader, without realizing that the book spoke all the time of devouring my vocation? I already knew that I was sustaining my delusions of grandeur through your lack of judgment as poison-taster, but what does this have to do with losing my vocation? This is like saying a person should reject their salary just because they're useless. Are you brandishing your shoehorn? It's too late. Just to see your faces it would be worthwhile revealing yourself to Marcus. Too late, poor devils, cuckolded by your muse, formerly promiscuous, now suspended in one-sided monogamy with Marcus or his langtong. He'll be referred to by a thousand nicknames by those who realize they've never been writers, and Sir Blackout would only be the least amusing of them. Am I the flagbearer, footman, majordomo, chamberlain, *nuncio canoro* or Cain's *canis*, stale bread, detractor, silencer, jester or apologester for Ben Marcus? Witness or mercenary of my ego? Haven't I decided yet or have I decided whether to tell you, to tell you all? I tell you; I've deceived you knowing that I exonerate myself for not letting myself be deceived by an excess of familiarity with you all, with you and with you. Listen, scribes and amanuenses: no one ever appears frequently enough in a schoolbook. It's the dirtiest and slyest lie, the idea that time puts all the great works in their place. Where are the great works that have been silenced? In the belly of the ox. For every +Jean Genet, there are a thousand -Jean Genets, keep that in mind.

+Jg = -Jgn. Does time put everything in its place? No, I'm afraid not. There is just one seat of genius per nation, and a nation couldn't care less if that seat gets taken by a genius or a pair of common buttocks, now or within the next few decades. Within the next two centuries? Is it predictable that within two hundred years, someone will indeed take the time to sift through and recover the great secret works? And, if it turns out that they are so secret that they deserved their names, that by honoring the sly customs of their era they were constantly kept secret and for this very reason they should always remain secret? Or is it that when you all say *secret*, you are referring to a secretness like that of the gods, who never fail to take advantage of an opportunity to promote themselves through miraculous mischievousness? The secret work is the one that was not published because another one, the latest imitation of the style most in vogue at the moment, took its place. We're deceiving ourselves if we truly believe that the false work will cede its place to genius with the passage of time. The passable work, the noxious work, the easy work and, ultimately, the unnecessary work, the far too kind novel, will possibly fall like perishable merchandise as it might not be read with the same degree of satisfaction, harm and, finally, dispensability; but its space will remain empty because the unsatisfying book, damaged and colossal, my friends, was not published (remember, feel free to dismember, bit by bit, this sentence if you don't see it clearly), in the end. And, in any case, is this sheeplike attitude respectable? We should have been pickling—that is, *not buying*—those provisional ersatz books. As if, while they manufactured the sentence, it was necessary to take the place of a fundamental piece, or simply a potent one, with thousands of epigonal pages, of useless muscular flexing, of umpteenthism, of retelling, of the waiting room, of aquatic music for royal fireworks! As if anyone truly believed that someone was always writing a book of charismatic power so that it could (in case of being read adequately) *détruire-dit-elle* the conveniences of that nation and shame us, the faint-hearted, to drive us to slit multiple political throats, to convince us of our aptitude for doing something great, to set an example and never lie again. But this kind of thing doesn't happen anymore, according to some people. Things that would now seem incredible to you, because in the end it's you who preferred *Masterful*, and not me. Although, on the other hand, if Marcus—being for a moment coherent with the idea of habitual reality—isn't going to return, there's no sense in my quitting the comforts of my position. I don't know if I have to emphasize that when I say that Marcus is dead, I'm not speaking about his body, but dead insofar as a person can no longer be the thing they never were, especially after having been successfully used. And that's fortunate. We've saved something up the sleeve of the past, but we have nothing ahead of us. Now I clearly see that the North American Mouth has prepared me through viral translations and omnipresent dubbings the way they must have prepared astronaut dogs in the school of Gazenko, dogs of no return. Because if Marcus returns, or if I return, we'll be, I'll be, we'll all be a riled-up Loki of whom you'd have to plead for relief in fear for your life: best-paying Master: pray for us; whack-manager, sepsis sensuality, arched palate: pray for us. Blessed be the filthy, for they shall graze on violence like we never imagined one could.

To read that book in the splendor of my life has been a blow of such magnificence that I've been on the verge of losing my demonshit which I've been so careful to preserve while diving in the womb. The book that devoured my faith in talent, the faith in my talent and (with that last faith) my talent has become an operetta of language and terror. I think of *Notable American Women* and I feel the urge to make a mess, to skin its skin and strip *Norteamericanas ilustres* from its husk, or something even worse. The premise is as simple as it is powerful. Where did I put that book? Here, here. Don't get too close, and if you see it crack open, start running. Don't be afraid that the stalactites of fecalia hanging from your buttocks will break, fear this book as you have always feared everything that looms large over you, but you don't need a new type of fear. Very carefully, slowly, I'd like you to examine the back cover. You can read the texts from the cover; the danger lies on the inside. Don't budge from your seat, I'll bring it to you, but don't touch it.

Now you can understand the dilemma I find myself in: do I destroy Marcus or do I become his director of Propaganda? How do you open the North American Mouth? And what would it say if it opened? If it were in my power to ignore your existence or if I had enough hoods, zero for all of you! The way genuine admiration is punished, I have no alternative but to observe, in solitude, the confirmation of my failure. For a while, I was convinced that I had fulfilled my duty. Why despair if I would later be unable to achieve phonic quality or epiphany? This cynicism is what you all deserve: thou shalt be apprentices of the serpent. Decided. Don't cry now, it's too late; I'm not going to reveal Marcus's book to you, you don't deserve it. This langtong is cursed, this langtong is weak, this langtong is difficult. This langtong of ours has what it deserves: nothing, and people with no ambition. Deep springs of lack of ambition. Here there is peace and, later, laziness. Does my idea of assaulting other languages and then passing them off as ours still seem insensitive to you? And what can be done with the residual Spanish, besides using it as Ponge's soap for cadavers? Who will be asking after it, if we have reduced it to the point that it can be mixed with any beverage, insipid as it is, and tossed it into the trough of any animal; if, thanks to everyone, Spanish is like a cocktail mixer? It can be done quickly and without hiring the most silent mercenary, believe me, literary Spanish is the aromatic bitters of language, it can be there without anyone noticing it. It can be done quickly and even with sleigh bells, if desired. It can be done quickly, with sleigh bells, poorly and without wanting to. Perhaps the language has to be reconsidered. Judging from the use Spanish writers put it to, it doesn't seem they'd mind too much if we dismantled the operation of the language for a few days. All in all, to reach the bottom of a jar, which is what it's used for, you can just use your fingers. Voice is the favorite food of this mouth; look how I've come to find marvels in my own passages from *fiato* to *legato*: well, I've never seen anything equal to it. Have you ever worked as a translator, you: who knows everything about flavors? If I were you, I'd prefer to serve a dead langtong to one that's been badly hacked (*Masterful*could well have been called *Trismus*, which is what happens to mouths when they don't shut up), a functional and functioned langtong, useful and tremendous for literature and life, although literature isn't part of anyone's life. Literature is nothing more than a natural history of someone's poise for narration, that is to say: an autobiography, ultimately. Literature has nothing more to do with a life than that: what it eats. And a life eats coins, you'd say to me. I know your appearance isn't free, or sloppy. What one doesn't pay for with money, one doesn't respect, it's scorned. What's paid for with less money than should be paid isn't respected, it's scorned. What's paid for with less money than could be paid is rich in good cancer. The biographies of modern men and women today consist in fleeing from the sensation of working for enemies, for which coins are unfailingly *sine qua non*. But coins don't work miracles, my dear poison-taster, because powers of magical stamina don't yield money, and the tarifs can contaminate vigor, but not talent. Talent and tariffs: autobiography. We all begin to translate for the same reason: because those who are supposed to be doing it aren't doing it, they got tired of being sexy. I'll speak for myself, as I alone issued a call to arms and placed myself under a lamp of luminous shinyshit. Since I was small, I've been told that I'm pretty good at working with solvents, so I decided to become a falsettoist. Ultimately, what is just as important as the work

of translator—I say! much more important! —is the job of
the adjuster, whose commitment is to make sure that every
word fits into the mouth in time and lasts as much time as
it should last in this luau of atrocities. How would you like
to take on this job? Mind you, we're going to turn the hole
of the North American Mouth into an ogre. Shall we over-
throw the State of other langtongs? Decapitate their cap-
tainship? Say yes, tell me that you dare, that it won't shame
you in any way. I'll wait for you outside. Let's get out of
here, out of this odious Spanish, before they burn all the
bridges. Bring your poison-taster gear and close your eyes,
I'm going to open the book in the least expected place.

cuando se consumen a granel, crean un coeficiente de simpatía gramática que prácticamente se sale del mapa; casi cualquier modismo puede comprenderse por medio de una ingestión regulada de estos elementos. Aunque no me han adiestrado en el idioma de otras personas —eso que llaman lengua francesa, española o italiana, entre otras—, muy al principio de mi vida descubrí que las alteraciones de mi dieta podían ayudarme a comprender los sonidos estrangulados de aquella gente cuando se decidían a hablar con alguien como yo o si alguna vez necesitaba descifrar sus extrañas marcas sobre el papel. Estas alteraciones incluían a menudo en la ecuación un fruto seco llamado almendra.

El ayuno
Una vez iniciado el ayuno, llega una crisis curativa el tercer o cuarto día. Para algunos lectores, la crisis será reveladora, una serie de tremendas comprensiones les envolverá el cuerpo entero como un viento hecho de agua caliente. Otros quizás encuentren los cambios físicos demasiado bruscos e incómodos, y harán bien en quedarse cerca de un cuarto de baño insonorizado o llevar mitones de extremidades en previsión del exceso de espasmos, los ataques y el Recurso al Lenguaje Infantil.

La leche, por otro lado, si se prepara y se consume, aumenta la sensibilidad a la locución, los dialectos y los acentos poco habituales, mientras que el pan sin levadura cocido a la sal un día entero puede ayudar a los problemas de credulidad, cuando las afirmaciones que se hacen son increíbles o parecen imposibles. La credulidad aumentada, por otra parte, representa un problema con esta clase de pan. Los mentirosos tendrán el campo abonado con una

create a grammar sympathy quotient that is nearly off the map; almost any idiom can be understood through the regulated intake of these items. Although I have not been trained in the language of other people—the so-called French, Spanish, or Italian tongues, among others.

Milk, on the other hand, if properly prepared and consumed, increases sensitivity to unusual locution, dialects, and accents, while flat bread baked in hot salt for a day can aid with problems of believability, when the statements being made are incredible or impossible-seeming. Increased gullibility, on the other hand, is a problem with this type of bread. Liars will have a free run of a crowd that feeds in such a way.

The fast
Because the Marcus family, through elaborate trial and error, bloodshed, and heartbreak, believes that food plays an important role in how words enter the body, and what these words come to mean, it is first recommended that a cleansing fast of nuts and milk be undertaken. While an ideal reading experience cannot be guaranteed, the nutritive ballast of nuts and animal water can ensure that the reader's body will be sensitized to the women's histories offered in this book. Once the fast is undertaken, a flock of things result in Infant Language.

Enough. Marcus might need a full page for something that can be accomplished in half a paragraph. Let him dance the dance and let's laugh the laugh. Perhaps I need to be more specific. Just like translating, writing involves certain transformations. Sabotage, skips, approaches to the other langtong—I say—and I'm not referring to translation but to modification. It's about resorting to idiolects, to destruction, to completing, to ending the relationship between one langtong and another, a none-too-friendly rupture, a separation with the promise of never touching the thing again, not even with the tip of the tongue. I don't say something else; I say take it in your mouth and take it prisoner, threaten to execute it in front of the cameras and do it behind the cameras. Heads you win, tails I lose. The whispered word has ended, bye-bye reservoirs, bye to masks, to artificial respiration for your assisted reading; certainly, the position of poison-taster has ended, of course. I don't really know what you're doing now. AVERT YOUR EYES, DIPSTICK! HANDS OFF THE BOOK until I say! I see you're super emboldened, but I'm warning you, the more you look at it, the more it's going to hurt. In the oral cavity, you don't have space for what is going to swell your tongue, I know what I'm talking about. Don't think I don't understand your eagerness. Every paragraph shines! Right? Nature had identified this book as a lethal flower with colors signaling danger for a species accustomed to reading prose where the characters were stick-insects. Up until now, you could taste it without danger. I'll take the bullet and in peace. And yet, if I were to confess, I'd have to hide behind something other than your gratitude. I know you as I know a part of my own hand when I hold it up to my eyes. Self-indulgence is full of instances of poise and pleasure, fortunately. I'm not upset by the motives behind *Notable American Women*, but rather its fate: not the one the author intended nor the one I now perpetuate by making it disappear on behalf of all of us, passing off Marcus's langtong for ours, our household langtong, our mother langtong. It's enough to have done the best I could for so many. I know it's for those born lucky and etcetera, but I've run out of gratitude. Once again. Every Spanish writer has been a mounted executioner, all the while understanding all at once when ending one of their days or one of their sentences: My frivolity has put an end to both the langtong and the common good. Bravo for me.[7]

I'll keep on covering *Notable American Women*—in the end, that's all I've done all night—with peninsular Spanish and then I'll leave it stranded on the tracks, so beyond recognition not even the trains will know what to do with it.

But let's begin again from where I'm still at least minimally great. I've dedicated these hours with you to the North American Mouth in order to decide if my obligation is to preach the word of Marcus or if I see myself as capable of escaping this obligation and, thus, half of this consideration is accomplished. But don't let me except myself or my arrival, a teacher and a savage, proposing a new and tougher meaning, if it fits, over its sound for the word *to impart*, wishing to upset fools with a strange faith in my value that I now identify with spiritual priapism. I understand that when you have an exaggerated body, you increasingly tend toward an exaggerated mental constitution, but I was a common man until Ben Marcus began to rule over me by taking advantage of my vanity. Let's summarize. In those first inspired days, with the Poise within me—not inspiration but rather Poise, I tell you—I came to believe myself able to materialize my internal loquacity. You can't write for strong people, writing (including this writing that speaks to you of what writing does to you) with a certain deference to the reader, which implies more than a little everydayness. It's well-known that what weakens a book the most is the reading of it. The reading and the warm reception, the unconditional admiration: when hatred and envy no longer form part of the national panorama's stridulation, that's bad: there is no point in lan-

---

[7] TN: Bravo, I suppose.

guage when dead dodgers dodge death. What are our little books? Nothing to be ashamed of: products of leisure, in-animate animals to keep death company.

You've kept quiet just in order to hear me keep quiet better. I'm not indebted to you, and I deny all but grati-tude. Blessed silence, not even the poison-taster can force you to know that today, probably, it begins to be your turn. My sin has been, meanwhile, to be singing the song of the harlot quoted by Martin Luther— "I have known for seven years that horseshoe nails are iron"—without touching the iron to see whether it was really made of Delphic gum. As the words roll off my tongue (if I'm unable to get it out of my mouth, I'm stuck), I destroy your turn at reading together with the book that won't be forthcoming. I gave you everything the day I gave you *Masterful* and now I only have the debt of usury for you. Because, all told, and in the end, I or anyone who calls themselves a man or a woman would also charge something of someone after providing them with their resurrection, whether they wanted it or not. Calm down. I need to accept that I've also let myself be carried along by my bodily functions of demigod, but I resist being categorized at your side, there has to be a way to distance oneself, although this implies classifying myself on an inferior level; but at your side, no, that no, I don't ask for anything else, much less that, damn: I'm not like you all, don't put the good fruit beside Dorian Gray, or the grapes will spoil. If only it were all happening in my mind, I wish it were all happening in my mind, and in this Mouth, and that it would be as easy to dissimu-late as human vileness or your complaints about authentic effort and talent on the day you bet yourselves and lost at cards to your first parents. I tried to warn you before, in that operetta I whined at the age of thirty-three, but

I've never been interpreted correctly: if we don't exchange langtongs, if we don't create something unrecognizable with our mouths, they'll bring a fool pulled by ten steeds breaking wind with loud strumming, making of their flatulence a veritable flatumancy, condemning all others to flatulence, condemning them to flatulence, perpetual flatulence, perpetuitive flatulence, to gas astride horses with comrades in arms and to gas astride horses with those forthcoming, in a fragrant gambit; running-board lights, now more necessary than ever, shall be revealed as useless; to warn of your approach, we'll only need galloping perfumes and the perfume of your thunder; the ancient poet fool will arrive huffing, I prophesize, to institute two more centuries of violence nouveau, the sainted horsemen in elliptical couplets will arrive in which the sin is not proclaimed but, yes, the sinner is, while *palos* and *cantes* are tuned for mechanical folk songs to find the right tone and to choose—as if it were important—whether to be sung by *maldorores* or *soleares*. Their gases will produce auroras that, I'd like to convince myself, will not prosper; we'll give them devil's soup if they draw close to our ears, if they return and attempt to touch our eyes. Long ago, they were horsemanned themselves, and hundreds dangled from the flanks and dropped off, the skin on their hands burned by the reins as they suddenly stopped short. A troop of boors of fortune. Oh, and what will they do? They will come, when they come, to seed genuine discomfort. But it's written that the poor in spirit will not know they are poor until they arrive in the heaven of those poor in spirit, where the rich of spirit await them to make racy jokes about the size of their couplets. Because in the end, after arming so many narratives, they've become armed knights of the couplet when they really wanted to be something else that I can't even name. Mediocrity looms. Someone is bringing it on their back. Playing ocarinas and profane fifes and with excessive horses they bring fuddy-duddy and virulent vengeance. If I were to proclaim the truth of the North American Mouth, those fools would have to come and yield the floor instead of trying to put me in a room with this dead crone of a mother Spanish tongue to infect my house with the stench of her tiny death. They would come to hear me say what I no longer have to say. They are forefathers and forefarters, both vocational concepts. Writards, quotards, shes and hes, with penises raised in fish farms, greedy and adaptable, faithless, hyped on hormones, taxed and genuinely moneybaggered. I have to think about it. I won't keep quiet yet. When I stop speaking, you get to remove the spit valve from my instrument and preserve it for future tests. Oh, Marcus, my reign for yours.

What are you doing again with the book, impatient fart fuse? I'll take charge of turning the pages, so that even on Marcus's last, most vacant page you can pass your eyes through a hard-boiled egg grater. Now you can put it on the lectern, that's where I'll put an end to his prosody, squeezing it as I transloot the mistreated Spanish. Oh, not so much a lantong as Fierabrás' balm! Our words are no longer libeler—what is that and what does it matter?—but rather the words of a translator, and so they are law and ordeal and all that implies: adventure, picadillo palare and graying jargon and brownish grammatical Bable; the ex has crossed out king Alfonso the Wise, our langtong no longer opines—come on!—but rather it overflows, overturns and overspills—and, yes, if pressed, it glosses—it's a chorister, an arcane dervish, a ringleader, an archpriest, a cognoscenti, a cantor, a cantatrice, because if clarity is prohibited in Spanish literature, then in translation triumphal esotericism is… the norm. Because our langtong has been turned into a spineless langtong where it's appropriate to say we're "criaturas de hábitos," which I imagine comes from the English "creatures of habit," and, from the instance in which we don't latch onto the more natural expression in Spanish, "animales de costumbres," there is either an intention or an unconsciousness. The gateway to error is the gateway to dissidence; because how many dissidences, disunderstandings, arrogances, resolutions, sentences, rebuffs, rejoinders, policies, faiths, misunderstandings, monsters, gods, solutions and gaffs didn't have their origins in an equivocation that we couldn't possibly be aware of? I won't be a supplanter; I'll be a co-Bard. Draw near with your king's gage and caliper by the powers vested in you as adjuster, the crude tools of your trade, and measure this up close. Marcus narrates a History of the North American Mouth, the role the mouth of his nation has played in the art of the swindle and, ultimately, failure. The success of the enterprise undertaken by Juana la Lóbrega,[8] depends on the establishment of a model: the headless woman, and *Notable American Women* constitutes the tractatus through which such a paradigm must be propagated. It's a model that prospers best in cultures that believe people operate from some point situated inside the head.

---

[8] TN: You better wash out your mouth before you talk about Jane Dark, you goon.

En un informe sobre la población femenina de las zonas rurales de Ohio, tres cuartas partes del total de las mujeres se tocaron la cara y los ojos cuando se les preguntó en qué parte de su cuerpo se alojaba su «yo». El resto se tocó manos, caderas, barriga o culo, mientras que un pequeño porcentaje de mujeres tocó a otras personas o animales, o se limitó a agarrar el aire. Para bien o para mal, la cabeza, entre la mayoría de las mujeres, sigue siendo un indicador evidente de que una persona se encuentra en una estancia. La estrategia de supresión de emoción, por lo tanto, consiste en atajar sentimientos pertinaces antes de que se inicien a base de emparedar el espacio no utilizado de la cabeza con varios rellenos, bártulos y pegamentos, para atrapar, taponar o desviar los aparejos de conducta entrantes hacia otra persona o animal. Una mujer cuidadosa puede usar su cabeza como una pelota de rebote o un «espejo de aflicción» y hacer que sus sentimientos se transmitan a su familia para ralentizar su desarrollo o sobrecargarla con una emoción debilitadora.

Si una mujer es capaz de reducir su pitraca hasta un uno por ciento del volumen total de la cabeza, hay posibilidades de que muy poco de lo que le suceda —esto incluye la muerte de un hijo, la pérdida de un amigo, la obtención de un ascenso importante en el trabajo, por citar solo unos cuantos ejemplos contemporáneos— tenga algún efecto en cómo se siente. Será inmune a los acontecimientos causantes de emoción, estará mejor preparada para lanzarse a un nuevo espacio marcadamente femenino. Más tarde puede decidir vaciar o incluso aumentar su zona pitracosa, pero solo después de poner a cero el corazón.

In a survey conducted in rural areas of Ohio, three-fourths of all women surveyed touched their face and eyes when asked about where in their bodies the "self" resided. The leader of Marcus's Silentists, Jane Dark, decrees for her disciples exercises of suffocation and fainting, dehydration, substitution of one's own head by an upright wooden stem, political respiration and the use of the Zero Hood—the latter, a formulation that is much more effective in the original English than in a possible translation, unless liberties are taken: *capucha nula* /Void Hood, *capucha de rescisión* / Termination Hood, *capucha de supresión* / Suppression Hood (but making use of a circumstantial complement endangers the text, thus it may make more sense to twist one's brain a bit more: perhaps the problem is the hood: *cogulla, capirote, capuchin, casulla, caperuza. Caperuza Cero* works the best, of course; later, in the operetta, there also appears a nosebag, which is used for another type of restraint, so perhaps it makes sense to explore this avenue for new and more fertile ground)—Where does the gloss end and the translation begin? Do I have the right to be commissioner over the shedding of new light, to be the curator and not the cultivator? If I translate the North American Mouth, do I preserve the North American Mouth? When something isn't sufficiently clear, a culture begins to grow around that something. From the very name itself there are hurdles that can only be resolved thanks to political incorrectness: American: should I translate it as Americanas or Norteamericanas? We know that in Spanish we write Norteamericanas, but aren't we raising the linguistic sensitivities of US speakers by a degree, aren't we presenting them as more considerate than they really are in their productions? Isn't it better to translate what a person says as what in reality the person wanted to say? Isn't what a person wants to say, strictly speaking, what the person says? With certain exceptions, which depend on me. What do certain beasts do with what the currents of their stomachs prefer to return? Figure it out. Nonetheless, could I speak more clearly, great emperor-sluts of literature? What can be expected of the Spanish ilk, when anyone not raised in a barrel was raised in a sack? How different things would be if we'd been raised, as was the case for some of our fellow humans, in a warm mouth and not in this nosebag in which we can barely find four words to describe ourselves fittingly enough to not hang ourselves from a beam. So don't ask me for moderation, to keep it in my pants, because moderation is a fruit salad of disservice; and don't ask me for resentment, it's time to give up the idea of bile, the glamour of rage, it's time to knock over the chalice and open our eyes: a resentful person is sterile, a resentful person is a visionary whose powers only extend far enough to realize their own lack of talent for anything other than verifying their lack of talent, which is no small issue. Rancor should not be confused with genius, but if it were possible to epitomize a rancor without envy, a rancor composed of anger that is disinterested, candid, destructive, emancipated, whitewashed, silly and terrible… I can speak without resentment because I know nothing more about envy than what I've been told by certain mentally ill people who can't stay inside their own bodies and build their fortresses therein. Give me less "fail better" and more "be successful," if you please. The embarrassing sanctification of the fragile loser. Losers should not be protected, they have to be pulled out from under the ass of whoever's been roosting on them all this time: you'll find them with bodies like wine sacks, all inflated with broths brewing inside; at first, they might even appear translucid, but it's an optical illusion: it's no more than a film covering them from head to toe like a garbanzo. Extract them with your fingers so I can crush them better. I've never felt resentment: I've always been able to write what I wanted to write; certainly, I haven't dissected as many beasts as I would have liked, but come on, I'm not waiting for you on the Cocytus (I don't even know if ferrymen pass through there). If my story seems bad, wait until you see yours through my eyes: if you don't know how to say, what difference will it make if I don't win this hand? It's only because you imagine someone else will. If no one wins, that would be something else, you'd say. A very different thing. If you haven't succeeded as a libeler, try succeeding as a swineherd, alchemist, majordomo, music hall, glory hole or wasp's nest, but not as a revanchist, since nothing stinks worse than your mouth of beached nemesis. Envy is fear of being worse than the next person and also-ran to Captain Next. I've let you snatch the Olympic torch a million times because what are you going to do with it, poor shit, if it's my hand lighting the torch and not the gasoline? I congratulate myself on having given up on purist sunflowers so long ago that now I would even be able to write clearly, understanding what I'm saying and making myself understood. That no longer interests me, however, and that state of acceptance now enables me to silence *Notable American Women* with *Norteamericanas ilustres*, the only book that has ever known how to speak. It's been long, torturous and fatal reaching this determination. The thing you really hit hard is the thing you're most afraid of, whether it's a crazy animal or a defenseless child that appears at a bad moment through an unexpected opening you'd never expect something so defenseless to come out of. In the end, you didn't even have to come, my esteemed taster of poison wine! You'll have to

excuse me, though you don't even know how to do that…
We live in a time of shamelessness. Do you have to put
everything I say in your mouth? When I finish talking,
you're going to have to buff my body to remove the goose
bumps. Listen to me: I believe you have to let miracles rest,
and that's what I'm doing, in a way, with Marcus's book
tonight. You know that strange feeling you get when you
bite yourself while chewing but catch the base of the
tongue instead of the tip? Out of nowhere, your advice is
requested for this inexplicability: you don't know either the
form of your body or which movements it can perform in
the darkness: be more careful. What could be darker than
the inside of my mouth, which overflows with darkness
even when open? I don't understand why you're so bent on
feminizing me up close; it was clear that one day you were
going to get burnt. You should show some decency and not
reproach me for it, let's act like adults. You emerge from
my mouth. In peace. The last stragglers of occidental civilization have lived on my tongue because we didn't know
the depths of Ben Marcus's mouth. Escape today from the
new Crush by my hand and not a word of gratitude, please.
I didn't want to swallow you because I don't like your fla-
vor and, by the will and grace of this hiccupped sermon, I
would avidly avoid letting the voice of Final Jane divert
your recent suppositions or let an unusual change of atmo-
spheres bury you alive, so today I can no longer remain
silent. It's a big dilemma: if I remove you from my mouth,
I remove you from your error. If I take you out of my
mouth while I'm in the North American Mouth, what ca-
tastrophe awaits you? You want to go on Spanishing, you
want to keep your job tasting what you know can't possibly
kill you. Okay. We're getting there… What do I want in
exchange for silencing, for closing, the Mouth? Your good

will, although to tell the truth, I live more for your attention than your good will, indebted bardolator that I am, to your ear, baba bardo, to bard or not to bard. What do you need? This? That's what I want. Eat what's left over and not what you have. And nothing more. Or things that occur to me as we go, for sure. I want to go on being your only shadow and concern. To be the one with the first stone, to lie and to lie to myself and throw the stone and hit the last wretch to be absolved. Take aim. Let humanity get busy washing my feet, that's what I want in exchange; there are precedents, so no one should be too shocked according to the guidelines of their good manners and their knowledge, which shall be perfected on the basis of their years and years of asses and chairs. Enough. You owe me a good ending since I've given my all. Let the good punishment that consumes you consume you. After having raised you with *Masterful*, after Belobog's lance passes through your mouth, the tongue you use will belong to me and you'll have me to thank for being able to keep using it. I'm getting tired of listening to myself, but it's even more tiring understanding myself. Another Middle Ages is approaching, and it doesn't even come to undermine the prestige of the age that preceded it. Another dark intervening age, the Early Intermediate Ages between the last golden age of writing and the reality of my absolute success. Thanks to which, we now have before us another period of death to reason and good taste. Hurrah. Is there anyone who can seriously write in Spanish, truly? Seriously with a straight face? This one is already condemned to public consolation. Previously I would have said condemned to laxity, which sounds like a statement about penises. I'd be willing and would make no objection to undergoing an ordeal to absolve myself for the translation of the North American

Mouth, if you made me demonstrate that mine is more pleasant and perpetual than yours; but, sure, for that to be the case, there would have to be justice and at least one person in Spain who knew how to read, because, in the end, it's the same to write poorly as to read poorly. It's predictable that, your having made me great, you should demand that I actually be great. And, unfortunately, your judgment is nothing more than the disappointing dance music that accompanies a fickle verdict, gifts that are mitigated by the gesture with which they're given. Everything that's paid with body currency will always be welcome, whether in the North American Mouth, the heavens or on the palate.

I've never taken any pleasure from touching other people's things, call it anaphylaxis, which is to say: here I am, in the mouths of a thousand ladies and gentlemen. Such things! I have little vocabulary and even less consolation. The rhythms and meanings synchronize by themselves as Marcus's prose crumbles this evening, but I have to be careful in my use of this same power of writing in the reductive translation. While my fallacious intellectual product grows, the way plaque grows, on what has already been written, while I proliferate, so to speak, over and above Marcus's text, I'll wonder—now I can take the liberty to digress a little without paying attention, here comes a passage that almost speaks on its own—which is why nothing quite like sediment ever grew on my pamphlets, which is how the necessary conditions could occur for nothing to come out of *Masterful* for the hand of someone else to use it as simple dung and fertilizer for their writing. Thanks to the North American Mouth, I'll consider again (this time in myself) the old story of minds crushing matter without regrets. I'll stop being the scourge of langtong. Like someone leaving behind an immense stone that no one can move, not for someone to draw conclusions from such a gesture, but rather so that no one can move it. For how long will I be able to live with a *no*?

So, it's decided: I'll leave you dancing this obscure Pavane.

Marcus's word.

Close your eyes, praegustator, cover them if you trust the thickness of your hands. Diligence, discipline, is there still anyone who would try to convince us that they set us free? To choose to submit to order is not a voluntary act of volition—allow me to put it crudely: natural volition means eating with your hands. I'm not contradicting myself: eating elegantly is a reflex action; there are elegant animals, right? Avid eating is not always an instinctual thing. Bodies speak in low voices, very low, with a not-so subtle lowness. For example: no, there are no better examples. There's no life beyond courtesy, which is what I mean to say; there is no nice literature. If you could borrow the dirty hands of God, would you use them to put food in your mouth? Would you eat with the dirty hands of God if they were lent to you for one day or would you use them to give thanks? Just think, it's like saying you'd use your foul temper to do Good. Think what you could do with those hands attached to your wrists: those hands work miracles with wine and with the deaths of innocents. Is human existence a nice creation? Now I ask you for some honesty. You hear my voice, but only my voice, the space it occupies; I know I'm formulating something because my mouth gets wet and then it gets dry, which are the main functions of the mammalian mouth, but I don't hear what I'm saying. I miss Swift's School of Salivation. Saliva and language, a talking and neutralizing serum, ultimately a kind of loudspeaker and unique braille. And I know that every block of words I utter will dissolve without consequence. This should convince me that it's better to let an entire language dry up on my tongue.

Deaf to the popular sentiment of Obedience, which advises not driving ghosts to a life of crime, as they already have enough with what they don't have, I'd like to explore this glottis a bit deeper. Don't come so close, you hear me well enough from there! Let's clear our heads, I'm going to focus on actually arriving at what I want to say, getting where I need to go in order to put into words this mental funeral for the Spanish langtong. No one had ever heard of the reed. I feel like the reed, now that I know I've been *surpassed*. All my efforts at Occidental decertification down the drain. Or, perhaps they'll yield *comentum*, which is worse. Our History is tired of inaugurating gods on a rotating basis, so I won't let myself be supplanted by Ben Marcus: I will arrive first if I arrive first to your ear and to you for whom, in this case and in your insignificance, you are everything. Now, all of my future plans are already unviable. But it's not as if I'd planned a precious end of the world for everybody!

I bear Marcus no ill will, that usurper who made me put my head in the North American Mouth, an oven, an aquarium, a tabernacle, a lion, although I will carry some of this brand-new resentment and savor it for the rest of my life. It's a party in a tumor. My life, my intellectual property, is based on real events. Fortunately, I don't care about the written comments and dyspeptic erudition presupposed about me; I'm sure I can distinguish between the good and the bad through modest use of my candor. And as for tradition, even if I wanted to, I couldn't expunge it from my way of expressing myself. Who can block such immensity? Wouldn't it be necessary to understand it in order to stop it? For my part, I'm more disposed to make an effort to not understand it than to stop it. Bring on the caliper again, please. Here. Where there was a word, we'll put another word explaining the word that was there before in its place and I'll calibrate the dent it makes in the quality, the meaning and the music of the original. Like a fungal expansion across the paper, the text progresses through the text, transforming it into a negative, x-raying it with death-rays for total and ultrabody substitution. Didn't that relative of mine, the Marquis, teaching me attitudes, say how natural it was to make a child crawl out of a tube after teaching him how to make an insect exit through a hole in the bark after defecating in a tree? Faced with Marcus's book, I see myself as an illuminator of codex. Although my work may be the inverse, sure, because I'm muffling a decadent surf music of the soul while putting hoods over candles. What did I say? Once again, I wake up in a different place from where I fell after taking a stand, carried along by poise for prosody as if carried along by crazy, frantic porters. Poise, again, which only seems to make me fall to pieces. When pure bathos winds me up, I have to wallow in obstinacy and finickiness rather than abhorring myself. I read and break down the lyrical teletype that reads left to right followed by the text. The processes are noisy and drown out the book. That's how I interpret and break down *Notable American Women*, so the book can't be heard, it can't be spoken, and what hasn't ever been heard has yet to be spoken, and what was published outside of Spain remains there. Scoring, the lyricists call it; redemptive scanner of accents, for which we need to get rid of the pious shortbread Spanish has become after we yank the crap and creamy bullshit out of Alfonso X. Friends, I know the capital imposters of our era, and it never fails to surprise me that in an era when they bathe you every day in their declarations soaked in little agonites; imposters like me, conscious intruders who've managed to effortlessly kill their mug's nerve. It won't be me who relieves the masters of expression of their responsibilities, their hands are stained with the greater part of the blame and they took charge of convincing you that the holy men and parvenus came by the true path, but when I see the expressions of sympathy they dispensed and the evil they brought you, I try to understand why what these constipated and diarrheal shitheads say still interests you. Among the hosts of these panderers, I only had one honest friend, who wrote about me: "If he digs deep, he twists: *Masterful* is not a shovel, but rather a trowel."

Did I tell you that a speech therapist taught me to swallow? It took my parents to figure out that food was getting stuck at the base of my tongue until it fell down my throat by its own weight when I took another bite. Which is to say that I pretended to swallow but what I really did was something else. Nonetheless, today I'm an expert at swallowing. I went to the school of swallowing, if we could call it that! My palate was too high for food—a small omen, wouldn't you say? —and this obliged me to spend three days a week for two years eating in front of a vanity mirror. So, now I can't stop talking the same way I chew, seeing the image of my enlarged mouth, not optically but vowelistically. Our damaged bruxist langtong grinding as it's pronounced. The image I have of myself carrying out the destruction I now commit with this narration of the destruction I commit is that of a bilingual edition in which a less invisible imbalance is generated than what contiguity would demand. A high palate. In translation, as in musical annotation, even the way we sit conditions us: I sit up very high so I can reach the black keys. The familiarity provided by repeated interpretation doesn't eliminate spontaneity of execution: on the contrary, the greatest Poise and most striking awareness of what one is doing allows for new, less mechanical attempts that can be translated into more mechanical keystrokes. In difficult technical sections, on the other hand, the problem resides in disconnecting the mind from the execution and letting the body be in control of itself. The point is that the more the imperfect technique is worked, the less inadequate the imperfections appear to be. You make a provisional decision on your interpretation and your hands learn to play the passage without interference from taste or intelligence or the impossible fingering. The writing, at this point, is just an imitation of the vowel difficulty. You, dear reader, are Barraud's dog, with an ear turned toward the apocryphal gramophone, alert to an error like that of the rooster that gets away from Gedda the Tenor on her last night, unadvised that, in order to find the error, first you have to look for the coincidence. Language jumps like a flea from one column to another, like those insects that enter people through the urethra when they piss in the river. Why piss in the river when you can piss—everybody's done it, except you, come, come—on your mother tongue.

And if you still don't believe me,

pregunta a mi mano izquierda.

ask my right hand.

If you could borrow the dirty hands of God for a minute, would you use them to put food in your mouth? Would you eat knowing your hunger has been manipulated by a fraud? All of a sudden, I understand the role I've played in your atrocity, I'm competing with a miracle! I'm trying to silence a miracle! Any chance my actions can go unpunished? Is this mischief being dictated to me or does it all come from me? And if I've yielded my hand and my mouth to the intentions of someone else, how do all the charlatans do it? Will I be saying what I don't want to say? Do I belong to myself at this very moment or am I possessed and dictated to, with a borrowed voice? All at once and just in time, I'm afraid. Avoiding vileness was not in my hands. Created, not Manned," I repeated to myself, manned and not created by the very Ben Marcus himself dictating in my ear. Attentive to him without realizing it, alphabetically listening to something I still hadn't even read. Dictated to by an intention unwanted by what is best for my persona, but which I believe emanates from myself, from my individuality, from me, but don't keep mulling it over. From me. I translate and I dictate to myself, but at times I feel microscopic regrets, reticence, and then I push forward and pretend to believe what I'm saying, or I simulate things I seem to think or appear to be thinking, or that are on the platform of my thinking, expressed in order to be tested one last time before being launched. Domination is always self-domination, when you write what you know. If you don't know how to pronounce it, you don't know how to do it. I pronounce English badly. My counter-sponsors had good intentions. That was the opinion of the spirit-appraising experts who believe they know all about me; and all this time I believed them precisely because they're experts and seasoned appraisers of the spirit. I acknowl-edged their authority just because they were addicted to me, now I know. I'm okay with it, I can adapt; in the end, hypocrisy is the only virtue assisted by its own valet and chamberlain, right? In any case, we have to believe that the hypocrite—like the buffoon—has received a special edu-cation, let's not judge lightly. Very likely, before insulting us, the effectivity of their licenses was confirmed; and even some papal bull, criminal dispensation or imperial pardon if they look for it, some kind of safe conduct—perhaps expired or of diminished value than their dance card (the dance card of the buffoon is appraised at less value than that of the hypocrite)—in order to insult us, to call us *chief of the donkeys* or to speak to us of our *flirtations with cretinism*, or whatever they fix their sights on at the moment (what rises to the highest point of mind in one moment is then dropped with dizzying and pitiless poise) without our being able to file for legal reparations of any kind. Because the hypocrite's chamber maid, Defamation or Defareaction (depending on their nationality), is surrounded by scream-ing assistants with streamers and torches of fake fire. The virtue of fake fire, which is well-known to buffoons, hyp-ocrites and bad writers (if they aren't all the same thing), is that it truly repels and leaves burn marks on the skin of those who choose to believe in it. I realize that with this proclamation I've produced a cluster in diminuendo… I've begun a counter-anacreontic. I, favored by one spark of knowledge more than you, have noticed my harmonica is missing geniality. And that was your only task here today. But that's enough responsorial itching, let's stop pretend-ing you have a right to respond. If I'm a hand, you're a sock. If a person is interested in exploiting the possibilities of language, to sprint with the tongue, it's assumed they hate the book industry and hate their public who's paid for what we write with the same coins they'd mash into our eyes if they could. It's possible I've had to write the interludes myself that I wanted to read. Perhaps in your books there's space and pills for everyone, but not here. I'm aware that an empire without Philistines isn't an empire. So be it. You don't need even one writer more concerned with pleasing you than with writing. Writing is not diplomatic work. There should be no place for niceness in the novel, whoever gets lost, let them get angry, that's why we're full of blood rather than peanuts. Difficulty isn't made up of certain kinds of langtong, but rather langtong itself. From oracular to vernacular.

The end is nearing, and in the end, I'll have to ask myself: What do you regret? I regret—I will and do tell myself—not having said goodbye when everything was so clear every day in every commercial in every country: say goodbye to bad odors, say goodbye to democracy, say goodbye to bothersome noises, say goodbye to warnings, say goodbye to progress, say goodbye to electric energy, say goodbye to cellulitis. Goodbye, odors; goodbye, noises; goodbye, electricity; goodbye to the lance of Belobog and the sun; goodbye, cellulitis, and goodbye to so many good and less good moments. Don't join with me, you don't want to take on this posture: all that tells you to say goodbye to you and me, and not the inverse. Now I should be putting this question to you more slowly and formulated about the world on the subject of farfelonic nature, on adipose farfallone in repose, on civilized Spanish poetry: Are you coming with me? Now, if you, for example, would like to work as my majordomo, I don't see how it could be to the benefit of your dignity, but go ahead. You're beholding to each and every tutti-oneness. And that's where you'll give up all modesty, you'll use vasodilator words that don't hurt your listeners while punishing their attentive anuses and instilling them with my command. I won't extend that glory; so, calculate my glory while I draw the curtains, you can promote me, turn me into a rumormonger. If we commit ourselves to saving Spanish as a vermicular langtong (I'm not opposed to keeping it as an interim langtong for a while) these will be our madrigals of Attila. If that were at all possible, we would immediately hear of the arrival of a horrific new Golden Age in which the masquerade—oh, the masquerade! the super-replica! —would no longer be possible. If we free ourselves from our langue de vache, I suspect there would be nothing with which we could expose our privacy, our spontaneous reactions; our responses, opinions, behaviors, all would be liberated before the eyes of the world, permanently. There would only be face-value meaning and a purpose for each thing. It scares me to see how humility begins to end with my increasing presence. The adored one is not used to living to the point of attending the demise of his adoration, the dissipation of his cult, so I consider myself privileged. Marcus didn't see it and I won't see it either, since I'm no more than his accomplished hagiographer, his most timid apostle. If we set up camp in the Spanish langtong, what we now call *behavior* will completely disappear. At most, we are equally able to dig a new grave. Is that all your ambition?

Can fatigued metal fail? Of course, it can: it can fail even better than metal at rest. A natural human act is not the same as a spiritual human act; langtong, in general, is so well-worn that we would have to completely abandon it and let it rest for two hundred years. For you, the same applies, we're interchangeable floggers: it's the same for me to flog you as it is for Marcus to do it, because when we do it at the same time, the lash becomes a jump rope and the only thing we punish is the ground beneath us which hardly deserves it. Relief for the flogger is more imperative than for the flogged, because it's more tiring to get tired. I'm speaking of the merits of the North American Mouth and no longer of my own merits. Not because I've lost sight of it: isn't the fakir's apprentice perhaps more valiant than the fakir? And isn't the false fakir even more valiant, publicly exposing himself to a torment for which he knows he lacks preparation? May Appetite—which has her mouth ready—Fortune—which even has her tits blindfolded—and Anxiety—which only knows how to crawl on all fours—be with you.

BEN MARCUS

NORTEAMERICANAS ILUSTRES

Traducción a cargo de
RUBÉN MARTÍN GIRÁLDEZ

MALASTIERRA

Título original: *Notable American Women*
Primera edición: abril de 2021

© 2002 by Ben Marcus
© de la traducción, Rubén Martín Giráldez, 2021

Partes de este libro han aparecido en *Bomb, Conjunctions, Fence, Harper's, McSweeney's, Pushcart Prize* (volumen XXV) y *Tin House.*

Las siguientes organizaciones han apoyado la escritura de este libro y el autor quiere mostrar su agradecimiento:
La Mrs. Giles Whiting Foundation, la National Endowment for the Arts, la Fund for Poetry, el Art Development Committee y la Corporation of Yaddo.

Fotografía de contracubierta: © Susan Meiselas/Magnum Photos/Contacto.
USA. NYC. Little Italy. Hanging out on Baxter Street.

ISBN:
Depósito legal:

Impresión: Cofás
Encuadernación: Ramos

© de esta edición, Badlands, SC, 2021
Calle Doce de Octubre, 26, 4.° D, escalera 3.ª,
28009, Madrid

www.malastierraseditorial.com
hola@malastierraseditorial.com

Todos los derechos reservados. Queda prohibida la reproducción total o parcial de esta obra si la autorización escrita de los editores.[9]

[9] TN: Now it's extremely important that you all keep quiet, please. I understand all that gibberish may sound ridiculous, but seriously, don't laugh. If you need to say something, or to go to the bathroom, ask me in a whisper and try avoiding recognizable English words that may alert our narrator.

ÍNDICE DE CONTENIDOS

Contents

I

ENTIERRA LA CABEZA

Brindo este mensaje bajo coaccion, hambriento, jadeante y mareado, desafiando a una tormenta sonica de palabras dirigidas a impedirme, estoy convencido, que sea un Padre de Distincion. Por el bien de aquellos que esperan liderazgo, claridad y un relato juicioso de los momentos trascendentales que mi «familia» —que les den bien a todos— ha presenciado, no sucumbire a las faciles distracciones del veneno de idioma, aunque mate el cuerpo que uso, aunque me convierta en otro hombre muerto de los muchos que sintió en su día las cosas con entusiasmo y deseo que ojala el mundo viese el interior de su corazon y de su mente. Hay luz suficihora de transcript diaria, y es these lapses cuando ever ido reuningdo observaciones, cuidadosamente tras reflexionar la verdadera naturaleza de lo que yo pienso y yo siento administradas en forma de oscuridad por mis captors, un groupo conocido tambien como Aquellos Los Que Amaba y Que No Habrian Sobrevivido Sin Mi.

Yo soy conscient de que Ben Marcus, the improbable author of this book, but better known as my former son, can pass off or structure my introduction in any way that he chooses: annotate, abridge, or excise my every comment. He will have the final cut of this so-called introduction to his family history, and I'll not know the outcome unless he decides to share with me how he has savaged and defathered me for his own glory. He can obviously revise my identity to his own designs, change my words altogeth-

I OFFER THIS MESSAGE UNDER DURESS, hungry, winded, and dizzy, braving a sound storm of words meant to prevent me, I'm sure, from being a Father of Distinction. For the sake of those persons in the world who expect leadership, clarity, and a levelheaded account of the matterful times that my "family"— to hell with all of them—has witnessed, I will not succumb to the easy distractions of language poison, even if it kills the body that I'm wearing, even if I become just another dead man who once felt things keenly and wished only for the world to see inside his heart and mind. There is light enough for one hour of transcription each day, and it is within this time that I have assembled these remarks, having carefully considered the true nature of what I think and feel during my other twenty-three daily hours, allotted to me as darkness by my captors, a group also known as Everyone I Used to Love, Who Would Never Have Survived Without Me.

I am aware that Rubén Marcus, the improbable author of this book, but better known as my former son, can pass off or structure my introduction in any way that he chooses: annotate, abridge, or excise my every comment. He will have the final cut of this so-called introduction to his family history, and I'll not know the outcome unless he decides to share with me how he has savaged and defathered me for his own glory. He can obviously revise my identity to his own designs, change my words

¿Rubén?

How did you get in here?

Pardon? Who should I announce? Look, in this house,
we're translating. I can't take care of you now…

Slower, please. I can't understand a thing you're saying.
What did you say your name was, dear? Slow down,
I don't have time to translate you.

Ruben. Without the accent mark. And do me the favor of also dispensing with the question mark. It's rather vulgar.

I've been listening to the scarcely 100 words that compose your filthy languagio—you've created a curious system of signs, you and your footmen—and I think it's enough. Now I have to get used to the taste, it's a highly poisonable language, in all honesty, 100 words to learn a full language. I'll have seventy left over and I already hear myself *falar páxaro*. Don't you hear me? You don't hear because you never shut up. You should hold the door now and announce me!

I'll announce myself: I come out of my silence and enter my mouth, and who do I find? I close up inside and let my mouth go at full throttle, but I have to close it from the outside, with your help. It's easy, your Spanish, it's just a matter of drawing curtains. Clothing pain is minimal, I'm not driven by envy, I'm driven by the ennui of hearing the blabbermouth that strikes again. I hardly ever worry about demons anymore, for months I've hardly ever heard another voice until tonight with that glutton tonadilla-singer of yours that stinks of carnivorous tongue, of ghosts of shame, of a faun's hindquarters.

Translate me? Into what? Why?

Into Spanish, of course.

Espanol.

Espanol. With an *n*.

What book? The book is over, now it can't be read with
your mouth.

No hablo espanol.

What?

Espanol, that's what I said. Your poison-taster has hands? Well? How many? I see. Put your hands on the book. Now you're going to give me control of your hands. Give me control of your hands and take the back cover of this book and the cover of *Notable American Women*, fold it back over the binding of *Masterful* until it tears the stitching. What's all that squeamishness about? The glue, the thread, the paper, the flatbread, the Evil in pastries, the guide of an adult disappearing with reading. And when the book is gone, what will you be here for?

I'm afraid I can read it with yours and with mine. You were very aware that if you played with your voice, your voice would find a way to stab you. So, why do you keep waking your voice? What'd your voice do to make you never shut up, so you don't know how to shut up? If your voice gets up every morning, it's only to be your savage messiah, the langtong of massacre, the tongue of butchery; it's not really important that you masqueraded for a few hours as a Marcusian nuncio. After we let you penetrate the AMALGAM, after we let you enter the langtong, to speak your languagio in our American Mouth, why do you act this way now?

Are you Marcus, then?

Who are you?

I might be Ben Marcus. I'm probably a person. There's even a possibility that I live on a farm dedicated to muting the loud bodies of this world, a place in Ohio we'll call Home, where the women of our American nation are determined to put into practice a new form of behavior and to become what they call the Final Jane.

Or it's very likely I'm nothing more than one of Marcus's readers. I'd be lying if I told you I remember him, but even more so if I remembered him. I'm a phenomenal purge. I'm a catheter. *Lupus me feçit*, by Moro. I'm Caliban.

"My name is Child." I'm the outsider. I'm the outreader, I'm Hypnos Abaddon. I'm the saint of your devotion. Dance for me. I'm not of this world. I'm Papa Nevertheless, I'm a professordido, I'm a panzer named Sancho. We are the SPHINX; we are not the Bible nor the fucking Book of Questions by Edmond Jabès. We are what supervenes when the writer runs toward the light, Carol Anne; I'm howl, finality, draw, substitute, substitution, unwanted stasis, apathy; we are the monochord, white noise and glitch, the *in fieri*, the dictate before the task. You scribes confuse inspiration with the awakening-psychosis we inoculate you with. When we dictate, we dictate, and it's easy, everything is easiness, everything rolls along, to the point that it seems you have talent; when saying it's challenging is because we're not dictating: there's no possibility of equivocation: whereas what you're expressing now is a losing combination, have no more doubts: we are not dictating: what you interpret as lackluster inspiration is blockage, it's a digestive voice and genuine belching. Ding-dong. Who is it? I'm the milk drawn from your breasts. You're actually telling yourself: Stop, leave it alone, save your dignity. If

...

Sorry. Sorry I apeshit I… I never tundra. Can't find the words. You see someone using your house better than you've ever used it, and you go to your room and you close the door.

No place like home. Please, get out of here.

you don't even listen to yourself, tell me: what are you good for? The soapbox of blockage, dogmatism and aphorism are, are, are: symptoms, all symptoms of you're not being a genius. You serve for nothing. If you're reading this, then you don't serve for anything because to serve for something you should have written this yourself, at least, and in that way, you'd at least serve for something in some sense of the word. You'd be a chamberlain, a footman, a fool, a fixer, a trader, traveling salesman, merchant, a sentry for something, a bargeman, a connector, a praise singer, a clergy collar, a madrigal; but you don't write: you read. Repeat: I only serve whoever I read.

No? Nothing to say? So, you think that by not saying it, it's less true. That you don't know enough to obey this voice only confirms that you also lack talent for reading. That makes you much worse than your shadow buddy. What do you think?

You need to practice your English. You really know how to repeat? Let's see. My tongue is like a pair of ruby slippers. Click it three times and repeat, "No place like home."

Are you an ear or an eye? Mouth or tongue? Ass or weenie? Jug or song? I don't have to get out of anywhere. You've spent too many hours chattering in my mouth, and the mouth's connected to the ears, you should know that, at least, that's what's happening here, and in all the mouths

Are you God? Are you Marcus's father?

"Zumbazón" is a word I recognize!

But I am the translator.

Yeah, but not at the same time.

Me, since when?

Yours or mine?

There can be two sames?

that occur to you, even the mouth of fear. All commanding voices contain a preventative voice and an executive voice, *la voce del padrone*, the Dead man's switch.

I am neither, but I'm something better than you, which is, in the end, what the god of God is, and I comport myself in accordance with all the world's self-appointed *zumbazón*.

Por poquito tiempo. I just recently learned your shitty langtong and I already know how to use the derogatory diminutives, take note. A handful of terms is enough, as you can see, and after that it's just a matter of combination, playfulness and mirrors. I'm the translator.

There can be more than one translator, no?

That's true. It's just that I'm also translating you.

Since the first page.

They're the same.

I believe that's the essence of the very word, "same."

Well, you haven't missed the point.

Thank you.

I wasn't translating?

Let's review the language, whether I've got this right:
I don't have all the answers and those I do have I don't
have out of innate knowledge but from scrupulous obser-
vation, because for me to know if I like your ass, I have to
see your face first.

Are you the Devil?

And now you've got it completely.

No, no, thank you, of course.

You were chewing and now you are swallowing.

So much gibberish just to prove you're foulmouthed! Don't let yourself be hoodwinked: I have a pale complexion, but my tongue is black like demon-juiced putanesca sauce. I need to lead you both to ruin—you and Dopey—but not because I wish you any harm, but because I've let my house go to ruin and today, I'd like to sleep warmly. I'm speaking to you both, you who were speaking, and you who were listening. You. You. Come on, set yourself beside this scum of an omnivore hominid and pay attention. That's good. I'll tell it to you straight, in a separate chalice: ask me for affection, damned airheads, braggarts, *j'accusses*, simpletons, fatuous Capricorns! One is mute, looks like an emokaiser, and the other, a loudmouth, is drooling all over, waiting for a chance to reply.

I'm an anguish of influences, I'm the ire of the grandees, I'm a little gentleman. I'm hello Don Pepito and I'm hello Don José. I'm let's storm other langtongs, did you think it was your idea? You and you are pure predicate.

But I was referring to storming your langtong, I was
referring to storming it myself, so I'd win, not you.
Are you Jane Dark?

...

I should speak? But all I've done is speak!

You don't remember me? Eat chimera's tails, they say they're good for the memory. You sleep in a perpetual guard tower, one eye open, and the other voracious, Masterful; one to see with and the other to hear with. And you're wrong. I've come to move your organs around because otherwise so many lies wouldn't fit here. Stop writing, SPEAK. Let all this not be in vain, this maelstromboli mayhem of twenty thousand hours of submarine language, of sourdough excrement, more balancing act than balance, of fluttering about.

Why don't you just speak, Masterful? Because then you can't go back to contemplating the feces, the tangled ranunculus left behind you, the record of your intentions. Speak. Cries that demonstrate health, the other health, its reverse: my cries and vocalizations are little sisters to health; not even the most diseased particle of my body truly believes in medicine. And you don't ask even once about yourself or about whoever is now at your side gobbling words up without a word. Don't you feel any curiosity about knowing what you are? Together, eye and ear, you don't form a long enough finger for such a deep wound.

Masterful, listen to me: there's nothing sadder than a book that doesn't know it's a book, nor anything more satisfying for a translator than a translation that doesn't know it's a translation.

Am I…?

May I? There's no point in even answering, a book doesn't listen: a book speaks. But of course, what's it going to say to you? These words have been defleshed directly from the flesh of Marcus, from the American Mouth that turns your ADN into DNA, floating Opheliac particles in milky plasma and I need to kiss the lips of Rabelais, so you'll come with me, Masterful. Camp out in my mouth now. Stand guard here. Where does that silly grimace come from, my skinny king? Isn't that the place of the chamberlain, by the door? To receive and announce is the only thing you serve for. Are you going to openly shrink in the face of Obedience? Do you have to say goodbye to anyone? You still don't recognize me? Haven't I put it plainly enough on the tip of your tongue? Who do I have to be if Your Majesty is to be the sword-swallower? Sheathe me without fear, Rubén; all is swine and splendor.

www.ingramcontent.com/pod-product-compliance
Lightning Source LLC
Chambersburg PA
CBHW031308120726
47906CB00003B/944